Last Dance With You

Grace Ingoldby, the daughter of an English father and a Canadian mother, was educated in England and Belgium. When she married, she went to live in Northern Ireland and studied at Queens University, Belfast. She reviewed for the literary magazine *Fortnight* and worked for the BBC, reviewing books on radio. Now thirty-seven and divorced with two children, she lives in Wiltshire and reviews for the *New Statesman*. *Last Dance With You* is her second novel. Her first, *Across The Water*, is also available in Pavanne.

GRACE INGOLDBY

Last Dance With You

Pavanne

published by **Pan Books**

First published in Great Britain by Michael Joseph Ltd
This Pavanne edition published 1987 by Pan Books Ltd
Cavaye Place, London SW10 9PG
9 8 7 6 5 4 3 2 1
© Grace Ingoldby 1986
ISBN 0 330 29589 6
Printed and bound in Great Britain by
Cox & Wyman Ltd, Reading

To Lucy and Tom

Prologue

What makes the eye slide? On that very first, cold, half-lit March afternoon Peter found something that surprised him, several pages of typescript: *The Journey from A*.

He pushed the chair away from the desk, his father's chair, his father's desk; he put his father's essay to one side.

In his life the old boy, Richard Francis Fox, had done many different things. Born at the turn of the century, he had abandoned the protection of school to drive an ambulance in the last months of the Great War. He had been late to go, late to arrive; much of his life had this quality of poor timing, arriving late, leaving just too soon. Consequently he went late to Oxford, he married late in 1937, at the age of thirty-six. Peter's paternal grandfather had discovered the Roman mosaics at Bignor, his father had become an archaeologist in his turn. History ran in this family like a rat. Peter, the biographer, studied the dates before him with a practised eye: Richard Francis, born 1901, died 1983, by his own hand.

By his own hand. Peter studied the typewritten essay before him. As his father had used the same typewriter for all his working life, the Olympic Good Companion Portable – and Peter could remember now the sound of the whizzing carriage, the tinkle of the bell – this essay, like the archaeological finds he was famous for, was difficult to interpret and to date. But the eye slide would not have surprised his father, for the element of simple luck in archaeology is, if not well documented, well known; things turn up.

The Journey from A began with an evocation of the sea and little ships, of fishing boats, round and safe in the oily, ropey, orange-peel, washing-up-liquid-bottle waters of the harbour, the waters which reflect the listed buildings which rise above them, the waters, almost stilled, almost completely encircled by the protective arm of the harbour wall beyond which lies the open sea. It went on to lament the land-locked life. Peter read on and the resignation of the writing scared him stiff:

I can no longer live in this fastness of gentle land and regular undulations. I long for the journey from A. The wind never brings the salt here, the corn and barley only mimic the movement of the sea. Only in one season does the sea cease to be this optical illusion, does the sea come to the land at the end of our useful lives, when the gulls follow the plough in late October. But, having flown so far inland, they do not cry or call but simply follow, small groups of large, white, silent birds . . .

Peter folded the papers in two, shut off the once familiar voice. His father had indeed left the land for the sea, drowned himself quietly in the oily, ropey, orange-peel, washing-up-liquid-bottle waters here described, had taken the journey from A. His bloated body had been brought back to the land to be buried in it in the Wiltshire churchyard a bare half-mile from the house. Could Peter go now to the rector and ask for the corpse to be disinterred? Explain to him, appeal? Say that he hadn't known at the time what his father wanted, be candid about things, be frank? Explain that he hadn't visited his father, hadn't seen him for some years – above all, that he had not been before in this, his father's room? The essay pulled at Peter's heart but he resisted. Like a dislocated thumb it pulled; Peter groaned and shoved it back.

The desk at which he sat was already littered with papers, the contents of only one drawer. A random glance showed letters, photographs and bills. The minutes from a meeting of the Richard III society which his father had set up; a pile of histrionic cards and letters from his mother's sister Audrey; an unfinished monograph on Eric Bloodaxe; notes on the plague years, 'God is Deafe'; a sheaf of carelessly folded tracings from Thames and Hudson books; word-processed articles from America on the linguistic achievements of the Large African Grey . . . What foolish over-confidence had led Peter to believe he knew or understood the man at whose desk, in whose chair, he now sat? Not his style, he thought returning to the essay; but what did Peter know about his father's style? The hunched-up figure of Joyce, his father's secretary, companion, housekeeper, dressed against the weather, passed the plate-glass windows of the sun room; Peter hunched his own form over the papers in front of him, a gesture part protection, part self-defence.

March 1983, my father's papers belong to me.

He watched Joyce from the corner of his eye as she huddled off with letters for the post; life went on, letters for the post. At sixty-six, Joyce, the baby of his father's dwindled entourage, looked older than the rest. She'd been hitting the bottle in the last week but Peter and Ralph, the old friend of his father's who rented the cottage that went with the house, both of them successfully pretended not to notice its effects. Peter looked out of the window for help. March winds had brought down the wisteria; Joyce picked her way through its branches where it trailed out across the path. Dark clouds massed to the east, oh dear, oh dear. Peter sat on in the sun room, chilled, unable to get warm. He thought of Joyce's hair, the dry, overpermed ends of her hair, rough beneath her scarf; it would rain before she got back, some consolation coming from the east. And Joyce turned to look at him, thinking herself unobserved; but the views from The Round House are clear and uncluttered, and Peter, with a frivolity, a friendliness he certainly didn't feel, smiled at her, waved back.

It was impossible to get warm. The single-bar electric fire, ignited, smelt of singeing dust and fluff, an awful fire in an awful bloody room. Quite apart from its contents the room was awful, marginally more dismaying inside than it was out. A nasty, breeze-block structure, an addition quickly ordered, seen to, by his father's unmarried sister Nesta, to whom the house had originally belonged. Peter barely remembered Nesta, only remembered her in an apocryphal, hand-me-down way. A tall Fox woman with narrow feet, marching about in his childhood memories with a swinging skirt and a pocket full of keys. Determined, manipulative and mean, or so the legend went, she'd built the sun room for her brother in the sixties – a place, in her house, for her brother to call his own; ordered, quickly seen too, built characteristically with one eye on the bill. The sun room tottered, thrown up awkwardly on the side of The Round House: metal-framed, plate-glass windows and French doors, windows hung with plastic, slice-your-finger Venetian blinds stuck unmanageably at half-cock. A studio couch spangled with orange and turquoise scatter cushions waisted with black plastic buttons, an ex-army desk and several tall grey filing cabinets, a sunburst carpet of such acrylic character that it would graze the unsuspecting hand or knee. And in it his father had lived like a pig.

Joyce hadn't interfered with the room at all since his father's disappearance and his death. No attempt at mawkish memorial, no pipe in the pipe rack, no pen on the blotter, no little tidy-round, no thorough poke-about. But then Joyce had been his father's secretary, companion, housekeeper, never in any sense his wife. It occurred to Peter that Joyce had at last distanced herself from the employer who had chosen not to see the writing she had scrawled upon the wall; it might not have been distance however, might simply have been drink. So this was a room without sentiment but not without emotion; frustration, personified in the cock-up of the Venetian blinds, lingered in it still. Slippery twin-lock folders tangled like coat hangers left too long to their own devices, an unframed picture of his parents, looking sunburnt, standing proudly by their bikes, dud felt pens and broken sealing wax, a screwdriver, a collar stiffener . . . Peter studied the stiffener for a while: what was it about these things that led them to make their final beds in ashtrays and the saucers of old cups? But the dressing gown that had slid from the wall cupboard into his open arms, the slipperiness of that silk, had

4

been awful, awful. A dirty, crumpled handkerchief in the pocket that Peter had held in his own hands for a moment before slipping it, guiltily, into the bin.

I used to dance on my father's feet, they were big and I was little, we went round and round and round.

What is it that makes the eye slide? The note on the chequebook cover third drawer down, *Must get Clem off my back*, Clem, his mother, sacred, sacred cow? Then a photograph of a young woman, taken outside a fish market and inscribed *Kate. Ever yours, Newlyn '78*, clipped to a handout of a beaming, full-faced Bruce Kent. *The Journey from A*, the feet I danced on were the feet of clay.

They expected a note, Joyce and his father's old friend Ralph. They didn't say so directly but like much else in The Round House it was circuitously implied. A note which would exonerate the two of them would be just the thing and it had crossed Peter's mind to write them one himself. He told them that he'd looked but come up with nothing, implied with a flippancy that didn't surprise them that in the mess of the sun room – the piggy mess, the chaos, the shoving into cupboards, drawers, pigeonholes and folders – that in extremis his father had been quite unable to find a pen. No traditional line of shaky writing, he told Joyce, no explanation to those left behind. No little arrow, sorry folks, no arrow that pointed clearly *This way blame*. Instead RFF had bequeathed the jumble of dismay, a cumbersome inheritance at once a comfort and a horror to his son. A life his father had been unable, or possibly unwilling, to wrap up. A bag of pebbles mobile in the undertow of what had been their favourite beach, pebbles that threatened, rolling, rolling, rolling, and coming, again and then again, again, inexorable motion, lovingly familiar, coaxing his little baby down.

For God's sake! Furious with himself, Peter shoved a pile of papers back into a drawer. *The Journey from A*, a piece of folded paper, no bogey. Peter the professional tried to hold these pages out from his heart but why, why? Was it the resignation of this essay that had upset him – yes, of course it was, this at least he was able to pin down. But why? Why did the essay frighten him, why be frightened when the worst had surely happened and there was nothing left to come? And Peter didn't know where the piece of writing fitted in his father's life and he certainly couldn't ask. Can't ask Joyce, can't ask Ralph, can't admit that I don't know. It was his father, that most intimate relationship, father and son, blood thicker than water, death by drowning, and Peter sitting there with a heart that sank.

In the evening he took the wretched essay to his bedroom and locked it into the case beneath his bed. All his father's papers belonged, quite legally, to him. They belonged to him, they were his; it was he, Peter, who had inherited the skeleton complete with teeth. But he could control his emotions; if he had any talent at all, it was his consummate ability to do this. He would stop reeling, he would draw breath. The following morning he was able to record his feelings in his old, habitual way: 'I lifted the mat of my father and found it to be larval underneath' – larval, how delightful the facility to be apt. A big boy now, nearly forty, Peter plumped, as he had often done, for flat dishonest prose. He had stopped reeling, stopped before either Ralph or Joyce had noticed he'd begun, stopped reeling in the spring of 1983 and begun, insiduously, to drift.

1

'RF was such a walker!' Joyce talked to herself as she laid the little tray. Almost a year to the day, she thought, but would not say this aloud even to herself. 'Twenty miles in a day wouldn't faze him,' she said instead. 'Enough energy for two!' A small pinched-up woman in her sixties, after years in the South-West of England her voice still retained that faint Scots something too unpleasant to be called a burr. It had become a habit with her, talking to herself, a habit, these disconnected statements addressed to the oven, to the fridge. The house and the atmosphere of gap had something to do with it, drinking didn't help; it seemed fruitless to elaborate or to attempt to connect. The vertical lines above her upper lip concertinaed as she spoke, then fell again, a fringe to her small, unpainted mouth. 'Enough energy for two!' She followed this one with an inconsequential smile. She had not walked with RF but hung about behind him hoping always that he would come back for her, take her by the hand. He hadn't done so; those hands which she remembered, large as sausages, working hands, always fairly full. Despite her efficiency as his secretary, companion, housekeeper (and how often this can mean something altogether else), despite the plastic bags she'd washed and saved, the milk-bottle tops in the Kilner jar, the small economies, the careful shopping — thinly sliced smoked back . . . the cooking — the cautiously boiled egg. Well, the list was endless: 'A selfless life'. The appointments book kept up to the mark, RF and Ig at Vindolanda, RF at Bignor '53 . . . So after the inconsequential smile the expression settled back into one of peeved, hard-won consolation. The house and the garden belonged to her now, she had plans for Ralph's cottage when it, a favourite euphemism, 'fell free'. Handled with care, gloved hand, her memories could just about be sanitised of hurt. RF was such a walker, yes, yes, that was the way. And let us now praise famous men, she thought, her heart quickening a little at the prospect of the arranged, yet so far secret, lunch. The hall clock chimed the quarter-hour, countermanded by the familiar racket of the well's electric pump. Two-handed – how much worse her arthritis had become – she carried the kettle over to the stove. Almost a year to the day, the day, she boiled the water for coffee for Peter and for Ralph.

Yes, it was almost a year to the day, spring 1984, and Peter was still in Wiltshire, still there. Slamming the stable door after the horse had bolted, deciding to re-hang the door, re-build the stable. The simple sticky business of guilt? For years, you see, he had simply written to the old man; he was good at writing letters, good letters which got him off the hook. *Lovely here in the autumn*, his father had written, *now do come down here for a weekend, Peter. Ralph would love to see you, and Joyce of course. – Actually I'm rather tied up for the next few months*, Peter would reply. There were versions of the letter that went on to explain in generous detail just what were the various strings that tied him up. *Come down*, his father had written. *No* was Peter's reply. Letters shelved the responsibility of visiting, that awkward-ness of meeting face to face. Ironic that after his father's death these letters, these versions of the small word 'No', had been indirectly returned to him. The letters and the papers, the piggy stuff, belonged to Peter, and Peter understood the responsibility quite clearly, understood the load – even as a child, he had felt it as a black dog on his back.

Peter had grown up in an atmosphere strained by obligation, compensation: the father compensating the son for growing up without a mother; the ingenuous son compensating the father for growing up without a wife. That seven-year-old today was a long-legged percher on the edges of tables, a man who crossed and double-crossed his legs and wiggled one foot when confined to the comfort of a chair.

Self-conscious, fastidious and fidgety, thin, a little raddled looking aroung the cheeks and hairline; the eyes, grey, the best part of him, but overshadowed by the frown lines on the forehead, the red patch he rubbed between his eyebrows which accompanied the wiggling of the foot and the crossing, double-crossing of the legs. In his year at The Round House he had kept his head down, kept his head, kept his own counsel, avoided conflict, avoided Joyce. He folded his arms, hugged his knees, rubbed his forehead and curled up tight like a ball in bed. Even when he walked, as he did now nearly every day – it was the country, after all – it was with a jerky, punishing motion, pulling sticks from hedges, twisting off old leaves, not saying where he was off to or for how long but simply walking away. 'The true pedestrian, the walking man': that's how Kate described him, Kate who had been his father's protégée, *Ever yours, Newlyn, '78.* Kate who might have been Peter's something or other if he'd known what he'd wanted at the time. Yes. That was how Kate described him to her new friends; Kate was very good at making friends. How Kate remembered the part of him, the cold part she most dreaded, how she drew him in her cartoons: Peter walking off and, like the man in Johnstone's poem, getting smaller all the time.

Kate had come and gone in '83 and, like his father, she too had left a muddle of emotions in her wake. Peter was no longer in touch with Kate, in any manner of the words, but he might well have agreed with her cartoons, described himself in her terms as 'a walking man'. On his own so much these days, he toyed with descriptions of himself – a habit which had hope in it, which suggested that he still retained sufficient interest in himself to attempt a definition, seek out a reference on the map. Presently he described himself alternately as 'emotionally incontinent' and 'technically dead'. He would say that he was a walking man. His life had been a series of stiff walks, an uphill path laced (like larval, he liked it), laced with broken bottles. A truck up a hill to a vantage point so far unidentified, unrevealed to him. 'I can't imagine any other motion,' he might say, 'one foot in front of the other, up and on. I'm quite exhausted by it, I haven't much imagination left.' That would have been a predictable extravagance but he was tired, unsatisfied, and he fretted, grown beastly in that empty year since his father's death, beastly in the gap between being emotionally incontinent and technically dead.

Joyce poured coffee from the blue and brown Denby jug – Peter had lived with her for a year – the blue jug. Into two of the blue cups – the blue cups. RSA exams, Pitman's certificates, the tuition of Miss Sproule and Miss Geisler, type to the rhythm of the 78 r.p.m. recording, remember always to ensure that the chief's inkwell is topped up . . . the cups and the saucers, the spoons; then she looked at her watch, settled the lid back onto the jug. A little too early yet for Ralph; checking the time on her watch, the wrist mangled by arthritis, the upper arm covered in one of the many cardigan tops of the knitted suits that had once been smart and comfortable and were now seated and limp – the cardigan tops liberally shed about the backs of chairs, the seats of sofas, throughout this chilly, unexpectant, under-occupied house. Beneath the cardigan, above the wrist, psoriasis, a skin disease dating precisely from the day RF had failed to return for his supper, crusted the skin of her elbows.

'Ah.'

'Friday,' announced Ralph.

The third cup was poured, 11.15 precisely.

Joyce patted the chair beside her, a needless pat; Ralph knew his place and also where to sit. Each day he made the journey, along the well-tramped path from 'his' cottage to The Round House: past the waterbutt and the stoop so green (and how often had he recently mentioned this to Joyce, the stoop so green, so dangerous to an elderly and brittle hip); not seeing the Volkswagen engine in the open shed that housed the Elsan, carrying the *Telegraph*, his excuse, with its paragraphs of interest to the occupants of The Round House marked off with circles of sticky biro; through the blue gate in the vegetable-garden wall, past the empty pigsty and a second generation of Kate's hens, through the bamboo hedge, homing into the conservatory, to Joyce and Peter, morning coffee, 11.15 a.m. Waving the *Telegraph*, jovial: 'I think this might be of some interest to the assembled few!' Ralph, who knew he had to watch it, living here on life-support. Ralph, hanging fast to the rock, safe because he knew the movement of the tides and how to shift himself should the water come up too far. He'd pass and point and comment: a ridiculous figure, ridiculously dressed. His coffee would be poured for him and he would drink it up, on home ground now, settling down again, assuming the expression of the dog relieved not to be kicked out at, kicked out, spooning in more sugar than was good for him ... Things had changed, but Ralph had survived, adapted. Things had changed, somewhat ...

They – he, Joyce and Peter – were the detritus that RF had left behind. The old days, when he'd popped across to have a pipe with RF, always something going on, things happening. A chat with one of the respective sisters perhaps. Nesta, RF's sister, Nesta had been good to Ralph in her way. The house belonged to her and in it she took charge; as long as that was understood, fully, then everything was quite all right. Ralph understood Nesta, quite admired her really; they understood one another – after all, it was Richard whom they both loved. It was the other sister, Clem's sister Audrey, who caused the fireworks in the house. Audrey was tolerated by Nesta, tolerated until she went too far, tolerated until it became obvious that she too loved Richard, she too wanted to possess him in her way. Audrey, who had that spark, that something, Ralph had once thought ... Well, he had gone as far as asking Audrey but she wouldn't have him, sensible enough. No, it was safer in every way for Ralph among the men. Ralph and Richard and their old friend Ig Wordsworth the historian, always in and out of the house ... The three men had been at Oxford together – 'Up together,' Ralph would say whenever he got the chance – and look, those really were the days. Ralph's interest in theatre had burgeoned there, such happy, busy times. Old Ig, RF, halcyon days, nothing to beat the comfort of old friendships, the two historians, Ralph the homosexual. Audrey wouldn't have

Ralph, and when the other two had married, naturally enough, well – it's always a breach in friendship, can't be helped. Audrey would have cemented Ralph's connection with the family, but even without her he still remained a part of it and that was the main thing; he was in on everything, then and now, quite comfortably in. Audrey's sister Clem had married Richard; Peter was their only child. Clem died – and this is going back a bit – a victim of the tug of war between Nesta and Audrey, Clem had died there at The Round House, a tragedy at only thirty-six. Now they were all dead: Ig, Audrey, Clem, RF. Even the students who used to sit there had grown old. Only the detritus was left, only Peter to bring the *Telegraph* to, and Joyce. Shame Peter hadn't made a go of it with Kate, just the ticket and not an outsider, one of them. It had looked to Ralph last year . . . or had it really, had it? What was apocryphal and what was fact? . . . Ralph pondered on, not deeply, oh no, shallowly enough to enable him to contribute to conversation if required to, do his bit when called. It wasn't easy living on charity, wasn't easy at all; he might no longer act these days but he still felt forced to tread the boards. His cough irritated him, he cleared his throat; he pondered as Joyce read the paper, traced the familiar path back into the past . . .

The present in the form of Ig's niece, Nicola, was due that very day for lunch. Joyce, without consultation with anyone, had invited Nicola to consider writing the life of RF, and Nicola, such pleasant handwriting, so charming over the phone, was coming down, was keen. Joyce didn't mention this, she kept it back: RF's biography, or lack of it, was a delicate subject in the house, diplomacy was the order of the day. And almost a year to the day, March 1984. Where did the time run to, when would it close the gap?

Peter drank his coffee, Ralph's ridiculous 'Ah' still ringing in his head. 'What's so good about Friday, Ralph?' he might have said. 'The end of a frantic, fun-filled week? Or is it fish, Ralph, is it fish? Do you particularly relish fish, look forward to it, fish? Fish means Friday and Friday means fish. Ah.' The stone on the chair in the scullery, the stone that held down the piece of paper which read *Three nice plaice fillets, please.* Did the fish man have nasty plaice fillets that he left upon the imprecise, the unsuspecting? No, of course, forgive me. Friday was market day and Ralph had a friend who sold legwarmers on one of the hired stalls. Frightfully popular, frightful: burgundy and oatmeal, lime green and possibly lime pink, Fair Isle, argyle, plain, stocking knit, garter stitch and rib. Out dashed the populace in their legwarmers, though body bags would have suited just as well. Country life: huskies and puffa jackets, barbours and body bags, stiff walks with difficult dogs, tall women with narrow feet shouting at each other through the self-inflicted deafness of their headscarves . . . 'Peter Fox is living down in Wiltshire, so I hear. His father died, you know, nasty business – suicide, I think.' *Oh, this way blame.* Peter liked to think that legwarmers, to confuse the issue, put the hat on it for him.

Nearly half past eleven and raise a cheer for the house that runs like clockwork but fails to tell the time. Joyce had her life now, at last and not too late: a nice fishmonger, a sweet little baker with a basket on his arm. Joyce the grocer's daughter, saved by RF the white knight, now bought her groceries on tick. The ex-secretary now coped with correspondence in her own right, and, had Peter known it, to considerable effect.

'Oh really,' Joyce said now, the mouth going up and down again, commenting on something in the paper.

'Hard to credit,' commiserated Ralph.

March 1984, almost a year to the day.

Joyce would struggle in the windy gardens throughout the afternoon, a woollen scarf tied beneath a woollen hat, a husky over her cardigan: 'Simply a policy of containment,' she would say, an approximation of the truth. Conversation, discussion, the conveying of information worked here in a circumlocutory way; complaints were conveyed via someone else; news, views, Chinese whispers, did the rounds. Her lonicera hedges had done remarkably well; Ralph had held the tape for her just yesterday to stop her stooping, he was so good to Joyce, so good: 'A good eleven inches in a year.' It was Kate's idea, lonicera, but she hadn't stuck around to see it grow. Still, Joyce confided in Ralph that she would, in all honesty, have preferred a wall.

'Who can afford to build walls these days?'

The price of everything was prohibitive, she knew, she handled the accounts. In 1983 The Round House had entered into a contract with Uneedus, a firm that supplied gardening boys, odd jobbers, recommended by Ralph. Joyce was far too frail to hack about like a savage; she employed savages to hack on her behalf.

Peter watched from the conservatory as this year's model, better than last's − all that could be said − turned up in his van. 'I thought we might do the first cut this morning,' Joyce was saying. The conversation trickled on . . .

They lived in Wiltshire but they liked to talk of London; way off centre, they gravitated with growing desperation towards the hub.

'Digging up the Circle Line again.'

'No!'

Well, perhaps there were ghosts beneath the Cirle Line, a putrefaction of ghosts, thought Peter, rather like the dead who huddled, squirmed, flattened themselves against the walls in the passageways of this ill-constructed house; even the Uneedus boy now struggling with the mower battled with the ghost of the boy who'd gone before. Peter passed him on his way out for a walk, threw a handful of gravel on the grass.

His morning walk: this country life, leisure without ease. The walk took him across the garden and through a small gate at one corner of the ha-ha, across a hard field and then up an equally hard and pitted farm track. The landscape he walked was bare, affording with its few and leafless trees absolutely no cover. The countryside − how he loathed it, a vile, an awful and an empty place, but better than London, safer better best. Splendid isolation and self-pity, walking forwards, thinking backwards, throwing gravel on the grass.

He had tried to get rid of his father, of course he bloody

14

had; it wasn't safe to cling to someone who loved you quite so much. School and university had been impinged upon by him, and later on Peter had found to his dismay that London too was full of his father's colleagues and of people that he knew. His father's life, until the end of it at The Round House, had been nomadic and far flung. The myth-makers had made much of this: RF the wiley gannet clinging to some remote, inhospitable but thoroughly acceptable Celtic fringe. 'What cared he for money not a jot!' – this was utter rubbish as any cursory look at the papers, letters, would soon show. Peter had read the papers, read the letters; Peter knew. Peter knew the reasons for the muddy fields, poky cottages, precipitous cliffs, for Hereford and Angelsea, for the return to Crete, the coach house in Penrith, the years in Newlyn: poor timing, large overdraft, an affair with his wife's sister. 'What cared he for others not a jot!'

Peter had settled in London. His thorough, solid biographies had taken up a wonderful amount of his energy and time, and there had also been a long running but half-hearted affaire with a Belgian poetess. London also offers four orchestras and a considerable number of public concerts, which Peter attended on his own. London had been good to him but not quite good enough because, however much alone, Peter had at all times felt himself to be unenviably exposed. Perhaps this was the reason why, at those concerts, whenever the opportunity arose, he kept his eyes tight shut.

In his father's lifetime Peter had felt as visible as a man in red standing alone against the skyline at the top of a hill fort. 'Oh, isn't he clever, his father's son. Look he's waving his hand.' His father dead was a different proposition; there seemed at last the possibility of descending from the heights and changing the colour of his clothes. His father was dead and Peter – how foolish this seemed now – had presumed him also to be gone. So, in the sun room, Peter had pushed aside the inheritance he couldn't cope with and completed instead the final draft of his own latest biography, *Old John Brown*. During the spring of '83, alternately lying prone on the spangled divan and typing rapidly at his father's desk, Peter had done what he was extremely capable of doing, had poked at, laid bare, untangled, whizzed through, someone else's life, but this time something had gone wrong. By September of that year his publisher, Hayward, sent down the first messages from the front: a long review of his book appeared in the *Spectator* under the headline 'Salad King', to which Hayward had added the exclamation 'Ho, Ho':

> At first glance Peter Fox's latest book appears as simply another adequate but unimaginative English meal. A salad, if you will: three leaves of wet lettuce, not even iceberg or cos, a slice of warm cucumber, the quarters of an unappetisingly pale tomato . . . But Peter Fox has changed his tack. Here he reveals himself to be an endive and anchovy man, transformer, magician, salad king. This book will be seen as a departure, a loosening of the corsets that have restrained biography for so long – a departure which will not, I am sure, go unrecognised as a first in the biographical world that Fox, erstwhile, seemed happy to inhabit. Whether this is fact mixed with fiction or that increasingly popular genre 'faction', it is a highly inflammable mix: one is swept along by the narrative thrust, pushed forward by the promise of surprise and shock, deliciously hoodwinked perhaps, but thoroughly entertained.

This review was swiftly followed by a glowing piece in *City Limits*. Peter felt by turns appalled and mystified by these responses, thoroughly confused.

'Passion and philosophy are the twin enemies of history.' His father had frequently quoted that, and with his father's ghost as company in the sun room Peter had fallen foul of both. If the public had been entertained at this departure, Peter, with his small resource of humour at this time, had not. 'Hoodwinked' was a ten-letter word most inappropriate when applied to a biographer; he had not intended to surprise, delight or shock. Poor Peter. Peter who had worked so diligently, Peter who had trusted himself to keep his imagination well in check. Peter with his arms folded, so scrupulously honest and true. Peter who abhorred circles, Peter of the straight line, Peter who had guarded late into the night, year after year, so vigilantly, against any temptation to flesh out the skeleton and so exhibit himself. He had endeavoured (and oh, he had felt quite the mountaineer) to present the jigsaw as he found it and not to juggle, not to preen. Peter the straight man, Peter the snob, Peter who was probably a bore, had been insulted, struck a body blow in fact. Peter Fox the Salad King, accused of entertaining, writing fiction, of making people laugh. Like the bent archaeologist, he had seen of course how a few simple additions to the uncovered shards might make up the pot, but a serious man – he was seriously serious – did not fill up the trench with fakes. Eight books in fifteen years; a dull but solid reputation, in tatters now, in shreds. RF the historian, Peter the biographer: the double act performed at a distance to a discerning audience of academic friends who couldn't get enough . . . Alone on the hill, Peter whizzed round the Circle Line as he thought of it again: South Ken, Victoria, Westminster; Embankment was probably his stop. The pyrotechnic possibilities of pen and paper terrified him now; he detected, even up here, a giggle in the gorse bush, a whisper on the wind: 'Salad King, Salad King, whatdya think ya doing?'

'If it's worrying you, Ralph, I'm quite willing to take full responsibility,' Joyce said, hoovering right up to his feet.

'No, absolutely. Up to you, of course. Far be it from me . . .'

Joyce extinguished the machine and wound the cord into an efficient figure of eight. 'It's the time factor that worries me,' she said. 'Time's pushing on . . .'

'None of us are getting any younger . . .'

'That's not what I mean, Ralph. I simply refer,' her accent with that edge to the 'r', 'refer to the fact that it's been a good two years . . .'

'One year.'

'Two years, Ralph. Two years since Ig's book.'

'Ig's book. I see. Yes, well, absolutely, quite . . .' Ralph stood anxiously in the drawing room, staying but wanting to get away.

Joyce, bantamweight, bloodthirsty, punched up the cushions to effect. 'It makes my blood boil!'

'Careful, my dear, let me do that for you.' Ralph lifted the chesterfield with some difficulty to replace a rolling caster and then moved off irritatingly in the direction of the door.

'Ralph? I do want to talk this out with you, Ralph? I would appreciate it if you would allow me a little of your time . . .'

Reluctantly Ralph came further back into the room.

Joyce, crouching awkwardly, now poked at the grate. A cloud of fine wood ash settled on the mantelpiece, window seats, pictures, shelves. 'I see it as a duty, Ralph. I suppose it's silly of me to expect you to understand. To my mind, it is our duty, our job, to put the record straight. For him, for posterity, for us . . .'

'For Peter.'

'Quite.'

What they were discussing, and had over the past two years already discussed at some length if not in depth, was Ig's autobiography – *nothing to beat the comfort of old friendship: RF and Ig the two historians, Ralph the hanger-on*. RF had seemed quite happy with it, Joyce had taken great exception to it at the time, and, as for poor old Nesta – well, she must have been revolving in her grave. Ig had made so little of RF's achievements, barely mentioned his old friend's contribution to methodology or indeed to his own considerable success. 'He's turned you into a laughing stock,' Joyce had told her chief, but chief had only laughed at her and at the book. RF had grown soft-headed, that's what Joyce had thought: senile dementia, a cause for the suicide – that and Ig's quite unforgivable book, *this way blame*. So now she talked once more of principles at stake, moral positions, the need for frankness and truth, and how she for one would not stand idly by . . .

With increasing desperation Ralph listened for the chime of the hall clock.

'An outsider was by far the best bet,' she said, referring to Nicola, Ig's niece, the lunch. Yes, she realised that Nicola was not a complete stranger – yes, of course, but that was her whole point! She was a different generation, she was a woman, a historian, hardly tarred with the same brush. Of course she'd considered Peter, naturally, but since the Salad King . . . The point was that she didn't want this last tribute interfered with, well, buggered-up by, any nonsense about RF's personal life – the affair with his wife's sister Audrey; no, Joyce would not be a party to anything that smacked of washing dirty linen in public, believe you me, but she thought better of confiding this to Ralph. Instead she insisted that it was 'time to call a halt'. Nicola was young, pleasant, sensible, serious and decent; she'd married Hughie Turnbull. 'You remember Hughie.'

'Do I?'

'Oh, come on, Ralph, Claverton's son, wee Hughie.'

'Did he have red hair?'

'Clavie certainly didn't. No. I don't know about Hughie, I haven't seen wee Hughie since . . .' Ralph was so exasperating. 'They came down the year of the beach hut, you must remember that?'

'Yes. Yes.' Ralph lied for the sake of expediency.

'Hughie is a writer of detective stories.'

'Really' – the clock chimed – 'I'm sorry, my dear,' Ralph coughed, 'I really must be on my way – '

'The point is – '

'Joyce, if Nicola is half of what you say she is –' Ralph sidled towards the door again.

Joyce pushing the hoover over the flags, pursued him into the hall. 'I can justify it on several counts,' she insisted, feeling hurried now and flustered, saying the wrong thing. Never apologise, never explain, she reminded herself. She could do with a little drink. 'I wish you would just stand still for once, Ralph, listen for a moment. You see, Nicola is a historian, not simply a writer. I mean, Peter's a writer, you see – it's not the same thing; you understand that, surely?' Ralph nodded. 'I've given the matter a great deal of thought, believe you me. Peter's not up to it. I mean, it's all far too close to home, close to the bone, Ralph, you know. I mean, even with the best intentions, you can't write objectively about your own flesh and blood.'

'Absolutely. Quite. I understand.' He did understand. He understood almost everything except why Joyce insisted on cornering him like this, discussing moves already made, cemented, keeping him late for his appointments, which in any case these days were few and far between. Justifying herself: why did she bother? It was beyond him. Used to authority, I shouldn't wonder, he thought, the secretary – awkward metamorphosis becoming the boss. 'The important thing,' she was saying . . . Well, it was important to him to make his escape. Why did the bloody woman go on and on and on and on? He had proved many times that his conscience could be bought; he wouldn't baulk at Nicola, what would be the point? 'Go ahead in good conscience,' he told her, thinking about his own, picking up his *Telegraph*, tapping the old crocodile hallstand on the nose with it as he passed. The important thing was not to be late today, to escape any suggestion from Joyce that it might be useful if he stayed for lunch.

'I only wish I hadn't made a previous appointment, Joyce,' he said quickly as he made it to the old front door, lest she get a word in, pin him down. 'I'm sure I'll have the opportunity to meet her many times again. Possibly she will still be here for tea?'

Joyce returned to the drawing room, poured herself a sherry, leant on the sideboard for support. Jesus Christ, why did she bother to talk to Ralph, what in heaven's name was the point! 'Loyalty' – well, it wasn't an old-fashioned word in her book, not at all. She took Ig's autobiography out from the glass-fronted bookcase and placed it on the table by her chair. She might need to refer to it when talking to Nicola, cards on the table, all that. She would have liked to scrumple up its pages, but worked now with balls of newspaper instead. As she criss-crossed the kindling in the grate, strategically placed the balls of paper, she rehearsed not simply what she would say to Nicola but the way in which it could diplomatically be said.

20

Ig had covered RF's life 'insufficiently'; loyalty was clearly, quite clearly, not part of his code. 'One or two tell-tale little gaps,' she would say, referring to what she considered to be a bloody great hole, 'gaps which, taken together, create an impression that, one feels, falls just a little short . . .' She'd known Ig for almost thirty years; how could he have done this to RF, to her? However, the biography she had in mind would not lower itself to Ig's level, that of scoring points. No. Written properly, it would reflect RF's true colours; nothing, directly, needed to be said. Any fool could see, even her hairdresser understood, how RF's involvement, particularly at Vindolanda, had been underestimated, distorted by Ig's book. The history of the dig that still continued to this day, those seven arduous seasons RF had put in; Ig, most conveniently, had barely mentioned this. Just because it so happened that Ig had come up with the trump card barely six weeks after RF had left the site – 'That's luck for you, Nicola. Remember RF was the intuitive digger, the spade work had been his.' It made her blood boil: 'I may as well be frank with you, my dear.' The ignominy of having to nudge her chief back into the spotlight, life was so relentlessly unfair! She wasn't asking Nicola for anything that wasn't her due, anything that wasn't 'fitting'. Timing was all it amounted to, bad timing – the dalliance with Audrey, but she wouldn't be mentioning any of that. Ig had taken over at Vindolanda and what happens. 'My dear!' Six weeks later up come the writing tablets, one of the greatest finds of the twentieth century, invaluable to the palaeographer and the linguist, and – who gets the credit, tell me that? 'Some of the few tablets now extant' (her Scots voice would rise marvellously on the word 'extant') 'private correspondence, official accounts, a new light on the history of the northern frontier 85–122 AD, proving that the soldiers there wore underpants and socks' – The gardening boy from Uneedus had laughed at this: 'Leave over,' he'd said to her. 'Leave it out!' The doctor had sympathised, the fisherman had been consideraby impressed. One of the great British finds, more important than the hair grips in the vicus, the Roman shoes preserved in peat. 'I think our task,' she might say, 'is one of reappropriation as much as reinstatement, don't you think?'

Ig's book was unforgivable, RF was a silly fool to laugh. Joyce wouldn't forgive or forget, revenge would taste delicious, and it didn't seem to matter that, now, he too was dead. A dose of his own medicine. Oh, but he was clever, Ig. Their nickname for him, 'the intellectual giant', had not proved so laughable after all. His sneaky, underhand generosity of tone, describing the worth of his friend, diminishing him with his careful praise. All that about Crete being his best book – just because Crete had been his first; the implication was that neither promise, nor potential, had ever been fulfilled. Crusader for the lost cause, that nonsense about Richard III. Richard Francis Fox had enthused two generations of students, a man of boundless energy and enthusiasm . . . She wrung her painful hands. Loyalty? As far as Peter went, she could hardly have done more; she would do her duty to his father, you couldn't do better than that. She'd given him a home, hadn't she? Put up with his moody ways, him and Ralph, both of them, for months and months on end. Neither of them was easy to live with, 'believe you me!' RF had left the house to her; she might explain that to Nicola, should she feel the need to mention this or that in mitigation. If it wasn't for Peter, the house could be turned to account, a guest house. Oh yes, and Ralph's cottage: 'RF always saw the cottage as a study centre for his students; a minibus, a warden, you know . . .' Oh yes, and then they would all be rich; someone else could do all the hoovering, cook the lunch and light the fire. No. One couldn't leave matters in abeyance for ever and Peter was not quite the man now for the job. Not like RF, not a bit of it: 'Such a walker, enough energy for two . . . My dear, how he worked, you have no idea . . .'

And as for the suicide, well: 'No one will ever know how I've suffered,' she would say, 'a cross I have to bear.' She'd taken it personally. Well, how else was she expected to react? He couldn't bear to live here with her alone, oh God . . . She thought she'd die when they found him, when they brought

22

his body back, drop down dead. Not for the misery alone, she had already proved that she could cope with that; no, it was the stigma of it, the public stigma, the awful, crippling, bloody shame.

2

Peter showed Nicola round The Round House, round and round; he wondered hypothetically whether she could be disarmed by a kiss. It was important to talk, about anything at all, just talk; that's what Joyce had meant when she said, 'You two chat.' 'You two kiss': that was not required of him. He talked as they walked round, as their heels clattered on the flagstones in the hall, on the worn treads of the narrow stone spiral stairs. Visitors to this house were interested in 'atmosphere', a situation now considerably spiked up by the suicide of its most famous resident thus far. Americans were best for this; they had big bums, which wobbled as they tottered on the stairs. Nicola's bottom was unfortunately quite compact. She was English, unlikely to get carried away. Nevertheless he concentrated on atmospherics, talked now about the quality of sound:

'It's an odd phenomenon, the sound of this house.'

'Really,' she said. He had an unusually quiet voice; she wondered if he was putting it on for the occasion — after all, she had dressed very carefully herself.

'Oh yes. It tends to linger, like everything else, almost everything, it lingers on. It carries sound you see, all this stone. There. Pan lid,' he claimed as a noise now came on cue. 'That's a pan lid. I know it because she's always doing it and I know the angle it hits the floor. Now upstairs,' he continued, anxious that she didn't speak now, didn't speak at all. 'Upstairs,' he said. There was no point in watching for wobble; he led the way. 'Sound is really at its best.'

Nicola mounted several curves behind him, hurrying to catch what he said. He stopped unexpectedly, holding onto the piece of frayed red rope which served as a sort of banister on the wall side of the staircase; he appeared to be contemplating it, he fiddled with it. Nicola's heart sank.

She'd expected Peter to be difficult, – she'd thought about it in the car – but instead he had been courteous to her, polite, almost dismissive, difficult in a most exasperating way. Men did not like handing things over to women, she knew this for a fact. It would have been easier for her if he had been difficult, and now she had the dreadful feeling that he was going to be nice. Nice and easy. How difficult of him; it put all her plans astray. Nicola had brothers, and brothers-in-law, a father and a husband, she felt she knew what there was to know about men and what was, in her terminology, the syndrome of the old plaid rug. This theory, that men were like invalids, got into a state, stuffy and huffy if the beef tea was unceremoniously slurped in the cup, if the rug should be tiresomely, inexpertly tucked, if due respect for their sickly position was not shown and shown again. Many men fell into this category and it was useful to have the ammunition ready, the expertise at hand, should one be asked to cope. A weakly species, a paranoid lot, who felt constantly threatened, who preferred hours of carefully constructed humouring to direct speech. Although it was quite possible for a woman like Nicola to purchase and put on her own pair of crampons and scale the steep north face, men like this preferred one to take the circuitous route with them, they wanted their arms to be taken for security and the bonus of simulated vertigo when one reached the top. Hughie, her husband, was just like this, so was her father; Nicola adored them both. Peter was difficult, he was not going to fit. She stood below him on the stairs as he fiddled with the red silk rope.

'Smoking. Out of breath. Sorry. Hope it kills me.' He breathed in deeply and they went on. 'Joyce's room is the best for the kitchen. Now,' he took her by the arm and led her into Joyce's bedroom, guided her towards the unused fireplace, huge and heavily mantled. 'Put your head up the fireplace, go on, you can walk right in.'

Nicola did as she was told.

'There's something about this chimney in particular, you're quite likely to be blessed by sounds of conversation, hardly ever indistinct but frequently rather dull . . .'

Nicola listened, hearing silence.

'The one in my room leads to the drawing room but nothing interesting ever happens there.' He stood in the fireplace beside her, looking at her; his glance was rather cold. 'No, really the kitchen is always the place, the hub of the house, where everything happens, don't you think?'

Nicola thought of her own kitchen in Eldon Grove, the meal she'd taken out of the freezer that morning, and the packet of Abbey Crunch biscuits she had laid out ready on Hughie's study desk. He always ate biscuits when he was working; she was keen to do anything that might help.

'Nice in here. Oh, what a shame, nothing. I always listen on the off-chance, never know what you might pick up.' He withdrew from the fireplace. 'You can come out if you want to.'

Nicola was attractive in a clean, English, upper-class way. Her hair was luxuriously straight and black, she wore a Guernsey sweater and red cord trousers, glistening little socks in loafer shoes; an Alice band held back the hair, which nevertheless fell forward towards a pink and white, determined and contented face.

'I expect the wind's in the wrong direction. Joyce talks to herself, you know; it's quite charming really, and one gets the feeling that there are other people about . . . Of course, when one is listening in like this, it can be a trifle suggestive, like table rapping, that sort of thing. One hears things that were probably never said. My mother and my father, I've heard them on and off, the talking dead. Maybe I imagined it. A house like this is always full of ghosts. Yes, I probably imagined it. Tricks of the trade, Salad King, all that. But you must agree,' he went on in that quiet voice, sitting down rather wearily on Joyce's bed, smoothing the bedcover with his hand, 'old houses have an unremitting edge.'

Puzzled, not sure if he was pulling her leg, Nicola moved aside, pretended an interest in the stone mullioned window.

'Houses like this are repositories, suppositories, depositories . . . of words, say all sorts of things never mentioned on estate agents' particulars or written down on deeds.'

'Like?'

'Here we specialise in single words rather than phrases — "forbearance" is a favourite — a bit old-fashioned, I suppose. "Loyalty" comes up regularly, then of course there is "fortitude" . . .' His voice trailed away but he picked it up again, he could be valiant. 'Have you come a long way?'

'Just London.'

The silence was lethal. 'I expect we'll hear the gong,' he said.

'I noticed the gong.'

Peter noticed the hairbrushes on Joyce's dressing table, his aunt's hairbrushes. N.F.F., Nesta Felicia Fox; everything has a story to it, inside, somewhere . . .

'Perhaps we might go down and see if we could help at all,' Nicola suggested.

'Yes, why don't we. Do just that. The crocodile was shot by Uncle Binks,' he told her as they passed it in the hall.

'It's rather fine.'

'Yes, isn't it. In those days one could get almost anything stuffed.' It might well have been his father stuffed standing there, the gong in his teeth. Peter smiled; it hadn't occurred to him before.

Nicola patted the old croc on the nose the way Ralph had done an hour before, a patronising pat for a poor beast, the gong suspended through the mighty yellow teeth, the gavil with a baize hammer end slotted in beside it.

'They were great preservers of everything,' Peter said, as if Nicola did not know. Birds and flowers . . . Joyce's rather like that really. She's in the kitchen, through here.' He opened the door for her.

'Thanks.'

'Will you excuse me for a moment?'

'Of course.'

Peter sped upstairs and brushed his teeth noisily into the stained basin, leaning over it and looking at himself in the mirror. This bathroom floor sloped drastically; he was too tall to see much more than his neck. He had been smartening himself up here when Nicola arrived, watched through the window as she pulled up in a spanking red Metro, noticed the way she yanked the handbrake – women did not use handbrakes properly, that was a solid fact. Toothbrush poised, he had watched unobserved as she got out of the car, stretched for her briefcase from the back seat, slid the Alice band back firmly on her head – watched her eyes take in the house, slide to, and then quickly away from, the eyesore of the sun room. They all did that, that eye swivel; another fucking pilgrim had made it to the shrine.

His father's manner of death, the death by drowning off the shores of the Isle of Wight, had proved, in its small way, quite a crowd puller, a temptation for a certain sort of woman and that peculiar new breed of intellectual feminist men. He had observed this phenomenon over the last twelve months. His father's choice of death site, when one considers the options, all the magnificent sites available: the NatWest tower, the Pagoda in Kew Gardens, weaving between high vehicles on the Forth railway bridge, hurling oneself over at Barnes during the Boat Race, going missing in the Barbican . . . RF's choice had a significance, a pathos, not lost on those who prided themselves on their sensitivity about that sort of thing, their understanding, their empathy with the tortured famous man. Old students had visited The Round House in droves last spring. Peter remembered it as a time of considerable irritation; he was constantly interrupted from the proofs of *Old John Brown*. It merged in his memory with the sickening look and taste of the coffee Joyce served on these occasions. Landmark, which came not from Brazil but from the local Spar, that tasted and looked as weak and grey as Peter had felt at that time.

Romantics had seen his father's death on such a suburban coastline as particularly symptomatic of despair. A man in his eighties, a man renowned for his enthusiasm, for his imaginative writing of history, his intuitive archaeological

28

digging, became in their eyes the wise old boy with the bifocal specs, the haze of pipe smoke (all apocryphal but jolly). Poor broken down old chap settles his affairs (should be spelt with an 'e'), goes off by train and taxi (they imagined Harris tweed and leather patches, frayed cuffs) with an apple in his pocket; he swims out into the orange halves, the Squeezy bottles, the old bits of broken tarred rope, the flotsam, jetsam, what have you, detritus into detritus.

Peter hung about upstairs waiting for the gong. Waiting to be summoned, he lingered on the first-floor landing, hung over the stair well, whistling. If Nicola took over his father, he would have precious little, little precious, left. He lingered, listening; only the sound of his whistling . . .

Lunch was brisk, the dining room was chilly. Peter, hastily replacing the lid on the casserole of peas, wondered idly if he should use it as a shield. But who could find fault with Nicola? Charming really, groomed for stardom, unflappable – the fresh face of an advertisement for shampoo, the refreshing quality of her stretching for a pack of cigarettes, as soon as the first course was through. Peter glanced at her and at the cigarettes, a crushproof pack, he could do with one of those.

'So you are to be the resurrection and the life,' he joked with her, as there had been no pretence of discussing it, no question that she couldn't have the job.

'Better than aiming low and missing,' she'd replied.

'Well. Good. Good.' Peter was quiet, considering, and Joyce asked Nicola whether Bourne and Hollingsworth was still there . . . His father lifted out from the dirty sea of plastic bottles and recemented onto a plinth or pinnacle; other, newer litter would form about its base, Big Mac wrappers, coal-not-dole stickers, pictures of Bruce Kent . . .

'Do go through to the drawing room,' suggested Joyce. 'Peter and I will bring the coffee.'

'What a nice girl, Joyce,' said Peter, 'a delightful lunch. I thought the fish was unusually good.'

'He always leaves me something nice.'

'Yes. I thought so. May I help with anything?'

29

'You could take the tray.'

They walked together through the hall. Peter, seeing the crocodile, remembering the hairbrushes, felt suddenly beastly and bereft.

'Joyce.'

'Yes?'

He put the tray on the hall table, took the finger of her right hand in his and ran it down the length of the crocodile's scaly skin. 'What's that?' he said, giving her back her finger, putting it up towards her papery face. 'On your finger,' he said. 'Dust.'

'Well?'

'Dust to dust, ashes . . . I thought we were engaged in a process of consolidation here, that's it, isn't it? The preservation of family heirlooms, the cleaning up of old monuments?'

'Peter.' Joyce's voice was nervous and sharp.

'We don't want Nicola to get the wrong impression, do we?'

'Don't be difficult, Peter, please.'

'I'm not going to be difficult. I'm not going to be anything. I simply just mentioned it in passing.' But she had passed him already; he followed with the tray.

In the drawing room he poured the coffee. Joyce's fingers shook as her hands cracked the cold dark chocolate which fell in slithers on the low, waxed surface of the table. He collected the slithers in his hands as the women talked, scooping them into a little pile, placing them, with care, into his saucer.

They went out to the car to see her off. Ralph, lurking in his cottage watched the scene: Joyce talking through the window (it was Marshall and Snelgrove now) as Nicola settled herself in the car, did up her seat belt; Peter twiddling the wing mirror without realising he was doing so.

'Do drive carefully,' Joyce cried and, 'Give our love to London.' She waved but Peter didn't; the red car sped away.

Nicola's husband Hughie would be sweet when she got back. He'd want her to tell him all about it. He adored detail and, lacking imagination himself, always begged her to 'positively' fill him in. His detective stories were vanity published; he did it for the fun rather than the money, his private income having taken most of the normal motives for working clean away. So she would do her bit for Hughie, and thought, as she drove, of what she remembered most of all. Well. Peter fiddling, straightening the knives and forks, smoothing the bed cover, so painstaking about everything, fastidious, rather an old woman, she might say. The grisly lukewarm lunch, the fireplace, the crocodile, Peter. The way he tugged at the cuffs of his shirt, cleared the slithers of chocolate into his hand, into his saucer. It had been remarkably easy after all to win the battle, to carry the day.

'What's Peter like? I gather he's been ill or something?'

'Fine.' Or would she answer, 'Convalescent' – the anxious mannerisms, the quiet voice?

'And the odd thing was,' she eventually told Hughie, 'that they both seemed more interested in me than they did in the book. Joyce asked me all about London; she told me they were digging up the Circle Line again.'

'Probably reassuring themselves that it's still there,' said Hughie astutely; he hated the country, the Heath was quite enough for him. 'Did you talk about the suicide?'

'No, we didn't actually.'

'Probably just as well.'

'It was a tragedy, you know. Does that sound silly? It must have been really awful for them . . .'

'But was it a tragedy for history, surely that's more to the point?'

'Not really, but I'm going to put things right. Uncle Ig's book was a bit light on RF's contribution – they were competitors, you know, more than colleagues.'

'Often the case with one's peers,' said Hughie, who knew this only too well.

'Joyce pointed out all sorts of bits that Uncle Ig had left out.'

'I bet she did.'

'What do you mean by that?'

31

'Vested interest. I expect they think all the other books will be reprinted. It's got to be financial; they wouldn't have asked you otherwise.'

'Thanks for nothing,' she said, but kissed him affectionately, beneath the ear where he liked it, where she liked it too.

'I hope this isn't going to turn into a crusade,' said Hughie, only half joking.

'Oh dear,' she answered. 'I hope not. Do you think it might?'

3

Joyce observed Peter, irritated almost beyond belief. Nicola had announced her intention of coming down for her 'preliminary week' days before; Jean had produced two dozen boxfiles for Peter, suggested a clear out – he knew what she meant – and now today he carried the boxfiles to the sun room, virtually one by one.

A cold wind blew, The angle of the sun room made it vulnerable; the wind shot round the curve of the house and rattled the metal-framed glass. Boxfiles were bulky, and Peter had to lock the door each time he left it as the catch wouldn't hold in this high wind.

RF was a walker but not a bloody pedestrian, Joyce thought, as Peter passed beyond the window yet another time. With relief she watched the final journey, watched him lock himself into the room and disappear from view; her arthritis was troubling her, her psoriasis itched so that she wanted to tear the skin with her fingernails from her elbow to her wrist. 'I'm willing to take full responsibility,' she'd told Ralph.

Peter had two dozen boxfiles and several black plastic bin bags; cautiously he edged himself into the room. Tracking to and from the room he had indeed moved slowly – he was in a cautious and a careful frame, going through the motions, taking it step by step, sensible and practical, efficient, technically dead.

He sniffed about the room, he frowned and peered; like a dog with another dog, he felt aggressive in defence. The boxfiles were empty, they were to be filled. Filled and the rubbish thrown away, filled for Nicola to go through. Peter

33

laid the boxfiles tidily across the old divan, his job was to fill the files, not to be sidetracked or impinged upon by the room; simply to open the boxes, with that snap, steel click, empty the drawers, the pigeonholes, the files, the cupboards, fill up the boxes.

Upheaval in this room, he thought, and yet departure had been so neat. His father had made a will, had booked a first-class ticket on the train, had ordered a minicab from Beeline for a certain hour on a certain day. He surveyed the tidily stacked boxes, the bin bags; he stood alone in the room.

'This is me. I do this. This is the sort of thing I do.' He contemplated the task ahead. What goes into boxes is the body not the soul, this is not shabby behaviour. All Nicola will have are the cloths left in the tomb – the dearly departed has long flown. He sat at his father's desk, looked sideways into the garden, immediately interpreted why, in a room that was full of view, why the desk had been so placed. His father's desk faced the wall and not the windows; outside, the fruit cage flapped ragged in the wind. In Kate's summer it had been green, and fleshy, laden with plump fruit. Last year Kate had given Joyce a hand. She would be out there with Joyce while he was in here working on *John Brown*; she would be stretching for the raspberries, stooping for the strawberries, slipping off the redcurrants with a fork.

Peter looked out into the wind.

'The last of the strawberries. The first raspberry. I'll pass one through. You've got to wish.'

' "If you don't talk happy, if you haven't got a dream, then you'll never have a dream come true." '

Greenfly, black spot, eel worm, carrot fly; whatever the detail, the women would advise him of it, would shriek the news, information, through the open window. His father had placed his desk by the wall as an aid to concentration – he would have watched a younger, less arthritic Joyce gather and trim and harvest in. Bottling, freezing, jam-making, jelly bagging – Peter understood the desk by the wall.

He moved to the divan, he held one of the cushions, winding the black plastic button round and round as far as it

would go, making it ping back, dent the cushion once again
. . . If you were so unhappy here, why didn't you say as
much? I had no idea you were ending your life like this . . .

*All fine here. Thanks for sending the book. Cherrington does
have a building called 'library', all that can be said. Ralph
says he'll read it, we can discuss it 'over a pipe', the heart
shrinks. Now look, do come down. Joyce is frantic in the
garden, looks frantic through the glass. I'm reading the
Russians at last. Dostoyevsky,* The Brothers K *and* Crime and
Punishment. *Today's stuff seems so slight to me. Perhaps I'm
out of touch . . .'*

Peter worked and sorted. His usual deftness seemed to have
deserted him; all fingers and thumbs, trying not to read
anything, trying to sort it out. He was up and moving about,
no point sitting there thinking like a stuffed dummy, hollow
man, old croc. Thank God for Nicola, because this time he
couldn't walk away. There were one or two things he ought
to . . . He owed it to the old man to . . . Where were they,
where were they, if he could put his hand on anything . . . His
father had three briefcases, and into these Peter put what he
could find of Audrey's letters:

*. . . you must be mad or joking. I can't believe your memory
is so short. I am not coming up, and that's that. I can't believe
you think you can just foist me on Nesta after everything that
happened with Clem. Honestly, Richard, I think you're mad.
If you want me you'll have to come down here to me, really!*

Postcards of hens sent to his father in this hen-pecked house:

*. . . I heartily agree that it is 'unfortunate' – how could you? –
that our relations have taken this difficult financial path but
you can't have your cake and eat it. If Joyce wants to start a
craft shop (how typically, grimly genteel!), you or she will
have to raise the money somewhere else. I told you I have
absolutely no intention of selling this house. I don't want to
live in Wiltshire. I hate your bloody house. The only way I'll
cross those portals, my dear, is feet first!*

Oh God, oh God. Audrey had never had to 'cross those portals', perhaps God had been on her side. Clem, betrayed by her husband and her sister, had decided to leave the little that she had to Audrey rather than RF. Perhaps it was Clem really who knew Richard better than anyone, who knew that her husband would put his work first, always, that he found shelter and safety only in that.

If you can't give me everything, Richard, I prefer to take nothing from you at all.

Peter willed himself away from this correspondence, which reminded him so much of Kate.

Don't read the letters, shove them in. The Cretan Diary, the most beautiful piece of writing RF ever did – out slid the dressing gown from the cupboard, into his arms again. Jesus Christ! Peter shoved it into a bin bag, then pulled it out again. He put it instead into the side pocket of the first full briefcase; it wouldn't fit, he pulled the zip on it, the zip stuck on the material, he yanked it out again, the sleeve of the dressing gown came off in his hand. Christ! He put the dressing gown back into the bin bag and was left holding the severed sleeve, left holding the baby – and the baby had been his, he had given it to Nicola.

No, absolutely. Take my baby, go ahead.

And before the cock crows you will deny me . . . Peter was trembling, he whistled, his hands shook.

. . . *I'm reading the Russians*, Crime and Punishment.

– 'Again he suddenly felt like leaving everything and going away' –

The sleeve went successfully into the briefcase, the correspondence with Miss Poppleberg into the bin. He went to discard the tracings, the old man tracing in this awful room; he kept the Birdlip mirror; Eric Bloodaxe filled two boxfiles. He couldn't cope with the photographs, they went into the bin.

– 'It was this feeling of disgust that seemed especially to grow stronger and stronger every minute' –

Come on.

– 'In a delirium more dead than alive' –

Got my feet firmly under the table here now, not as bad as I thought, you know. Ralph's about a bit, Joyce is capable of course.

Daddy, daddy, my heart belongs to daddy. The picture of his father that Peter had held for so long in his mind grew more and more vivid as he touched the things he'd touched, the life, arbitrarily throwing bits of it away. He remembered the business his father had called 'bibs and braces' of adding twine to the leather straps on his rucksack, the picnic basket with its tin boxes for sandwiches and cake, and the metal screw-top flask titled 'Spirits' which had fascinated him as a child. His father used this as a hipflask when they walked together, up hill forts, round hill forts, down hill forts, onto beaches. His father had been dreadful about beaches. Peter always wanted to go to Bournemouth or Weymouth or Weston-super-mare, but the beaches they went to put all but the most intrepid climbers off, involved careful descents and heavy walking over pebbles, always a better bit round the corner, around the headland, up here, down there, this way to the vantage point so that they could get their breath back, get into the lee. Peter walking behind the bibs and braces of the rucksack sucking an orange with a sugar lump stuck into it. 'Not much further now old boy, come on.'

Not much further now, Peter worked shakily away. He'd liked to pick the dust and fluff from his father's turn-ups; what an odd detail to remember for the first time now – does it mean anything, does anything mean anything at all? Peter dropped things, clumsiness took him over, pieces of writing jumped out at him, bogey men, baddies; he was sweating, images followed overlapping, he caught his fingers as he filled the last box – this is murder.

– 'It's red, and blood doesn't show so much on red. Good Lord, am I going off my head?' –

He sucked his fingers, he cleared his throat. A room left to its own devices rearranges itself to hurt again, not the first shock of discovery but the deeper bruise beneath, the permanent state – that's what he couldn't face about it: a year later it still hurts. He regarded the carnage, the gaping cabinets, the full boxes on the divan bed. Check the cupboards, don't leave any loose ends now. It occurred to him, quite out of the blue, that these papers, this life, might well have been collected up in this way some time before. History repeating itself perhaps, the pattern on the biscuit tin of the child holding the biscuit tin with a pattern of . . . Was that it? Was this how the mess originated? Had his father attempted to collect things up in just this way to give to him, to create some shape and form from this amorphous mass, this life, and then just given up, as Peter had felt like doing? Given up, returned it, stuffed it, shoved it, into the cupboards, drawers, files and pigeonholes? Peter regarded the collar stiffener with suspicion . . . He had achieved it, the cupboards were empty, the boxes and the bin bags were full. He hurried now, abandoned the boxes, unlocked the door.

– 'There was not a moment to lose. He took out the hatchet, raised it with both hands, hardly feeling what he was doing and almost with no effort, almost mechanically struck her on the head with the back of it. Blood gushed out as from an upturned tumbler and she fell straight on her back' –

'You shouldn't have bothered about all that,' Nicola said over supper. The evenings were growing lighter but still at 9.00 p.m. darkness had come outside. 'It must be gruesome for you, going through his things.'

'Not at all. I thought you might like to make a start straight away.'

Surprisingly she shook her head, the dark hair swung. It had been a nasty trip down, wet and windy, cars on the motorway, an endless and dangerously mesmeric stream of light. 'Let's leave it till the morning, then we'll both be fresh.' She was as charming and as good to look at as he remembered; her voice, writer-in-residence now, was firm. The child has a tummy ache but he really ought to go to school; the child mustn't be allowed to make an issue of giving up his dad.

They talked, instead, of Ig that evening. Peter told his father's much told story about the American suit. Ralph remembered the tennis game for their benefit: 'You played well, how did I play?' Joyce's pastry was leaden, her voice crackly and embarrassingly over-bright.

Later, when the house was all in bed, Peter walked about the garden in the dark and wet. He saw the light go off in Ralph's cottage, the light come on in the spare room where Nicola now slept. In the moonlight the sun room was opaque behind the Venetian blinds.

The summer his mother had died Peter had stayed at The Round House with Aunt Nesta and Joyce: Audrey and his father had been in Crete. He'd got stuck in the fruit cage, God knows how, his snake belt caught up on the netting perhaps; in any case, he'd been forced to call for help, and Nesta and Joyce had come to tug him free. He was sick afterwards; they told him he deserved to be. Walking past the cage now, he thought he had been sick with fear rather than from unripe fruit. And now the sun room was fear; in it he had moved from technically dead to emotionally incontinent: 0–80 m.p.h. in 15 seconds flat.

Not sleepy, he cleared what was left in the kitchen, washed off the breadboard, washed out the cloth he washed it with, Brilloed a little around the taps. The night he'd lost Kate he'd done that, delaying tactics in the kitchen, what a perfect fool.

Up the stairs to Joyce's room, where she slept buttoned and cuffed, self-satisfied in lavender-sprigged winceyette – the ivory-backed brushes, the spatter of talcum powder where she had done her feet on the bedside rug. In the spare room where Kate had slept the year before, Nicola looked at the latest copy of *Interiors* by the light of the anglepoise lamp. It was rather pleasant to have the bed to herself now and then. Hughie would cope. It was utterly luxurious to be married two years, to miss and not to miss him like this, to go away and work and to know, both know, that you were coming back.

Peter went into his own room, simply a step away across the little landing, went in and quietly closed the door. Last year he would have gone into the spare room, the same light coming from beneath the door, the door ajar for him. It had started innocently enough. He'd heard the sound of daddy-longlegs or moths hitting hard on the lamp. That first time he went in, October moonlight had revealed the mess of unpacking, though Kate had been at The Round House for over a week by then. The unpacking that a more disciplined person would have long ago found a home for, or the unpacking that would have been dealt with by a person who had definitely decided she was here to stay; the unpacking not even put successfully to one side that told Peter, warned him, not to read too much into Kate's stay, not to misinterpret her presence in the house. A needle with a blue thread stuck into the cover of a book – now really; two shoes, not a pair, lay abandoned on the floor. The counterpane trailing beneath the bed; the jumper and shirt taken off together and inside out were on top of the bed where Kate slept, in her own words, 'like a log'. He had stood and watched her breathing, seeing her hair and not her face, which lay turned towards the curving wall. And it had become, after this first time, a habit with him, to enter her room and extinguish her light and incidentally – well, it was almost as if she left it out for him each night – to read what she had written in her diary: that writing, strong and big at the beginning, the writing that diminished in size during her extended visit to the house. The secrets of The Round House had always been his. As a child, he hardly needed any sleep; he'd wander round when Nesta and Joyce had gone to bed. He'd touched the coarse folds of Nesta's dresses, spread, regal and frightening, along the ottoman in her room; he'd known even as a very little boy that creams and talcum powders were not the only comforters Joyce took to see her through the night. As a biographer, he'd been reading people's diaries since his working life began. Reading Kate's wasn't so different, was it? He loved Kate. He felt he had a right to know.

'*You didn't mind?*'
  '*I didn't know.*'

40

Peter's dream that night was the recurring one in which he and Kate were dancing.

This train is for Reading, Newbury, Westbury, Castle Cary, Taunton, Tiverton junction . . . St Austel and Penzance.

They sorted things out between them, they rode out into the sunset on a train, the train.

'It was the life in you that frightened me to death.'

'Audrey told me once that all the Foxes, you, your father, all the Foxes were on the side of death.'

Hot and cold snacks, toasted sandwiches, chilled drinks and the British Rail all-day breakfast . . .

The carriage in which they danced was strung with fairy lights; Kate, like a magnificent fire, massive in a bright-red dress. He held her hand and then he kissed her ear. He kissed the other ear as well! Santayana served sandwiches, chilled lager and miniature bottles of vodka and gin. 'An invitation to the dance is not rendered ironical because the dance cannot last forever . . . The transitoriness of things is essential to their physical being and not at all sad in itself; it becomes sad by virtue of sentimental illusion, which makes us imagine that they wish to endure, and that their end is always untimely; but in a healthy nature it is not so.'

Peter awoke. Joyce and Nicola were discussing curtains but in a different sense. 'I double-lined them,' Joyce explained – he heard them clearly, for they paused on the little landing at the top of the spiral stairs – 'Good fabric, double-lining and a decent hem . . .' Their voices, Santayana's voice, Kate in her magnificent dress, the music, all faded, the fairy lights grew dim, the carriage shuddered and then stopped.

4

Peter put himself entirely at Nicola's disposal. Work began. Would Nicola need another desk or would she use the long table? Nicola would work at the desk on the condition that it was moved nearer to the window, to the light; actually, she admitted, she often liked to pile things up and do them on the floor. This was fine with him, no problem. She asked for a wastepaper basket, a basket was brought, with a flick of her elegant wrist she permanently corrected the cock-eyed, half-closed slope of the Venetian blinds.

He was at her disposal, he was there. When she skimmed along her ruled feint notebook with the OI Edding Profipen, he put his head down and kept quiet; Nicola and the rollerball would exorcise the ghost. He whistled, and when he realised he was whistling he stopped. He hunched his shoulders and wound his arms about his body in an effort to look small. He was at her disposal, alert. She didn't like to say that really she didn't need him there at all. Her approach, like the mothers at the best children's parties, was enthusiastic but firm. That first morning she thanked him for the boxfiling, though it happened to be the sort of filing she couldn't be doing with at all. 'A terrific help, Peter, honestly, you shouldn't have gone to so much trouble. Honestly.' Like Joyce the words 'honesty' and 'truth' came quickly to her lips, but she didn't mention frankness, she didn't have that edge. She was clinical rather than ruthless. Peter was disappointed and depressed; he went outside periodically to whistle in the wind. For all their sakes, it was important that she got on.

This was Nicola's first really 'big' commision; inside herself she felt a joyful leap. It had been necessary for her to sort Peter out in her mind before she returned to The Round House to start work, and she had decided thus: Peter was someone who evidently lacked his father's confidence, conviction and verve; someone who, since his father's suicide, found himself at a crossroads in his personal and working life; a man drifting, a man treading water. As shorthand, and she was very good at shorthand, she saw him as the boy in the shadow of his father; she could certainly cope with that.

Respect for his experience, the solid reputation, did not stop her pursuing what she was doing in her own way, and he respected her for that. He drew her out on her intentions towards his father, and hearing her discuss her task and her method of approaching it was like listening to an echo of his own young voice, but this he did not say. Ideally, she claimed, she believed in good clean lines in architecture as well as life: clear the façade, scrap the facing to reveal the original brick, get rid of inessentials (Peter?), demolish the Victorian porch. Only when the ground was cleared could anything begin to crystallise or to form. She hoped that the work might fall under several headings. Enthusiasm was a key word for RF, vigor was something she intended to convey. An introduction, a beginning, middle, end and summary, like an undertaker there was a perfectly controllable end in sight, so – although she hated to do it – she was afraid she felt it necessary to empty out the boxfiles once again: goats and chaff might be concealed there, red herrings might obstruct her way. Starting from scratch – and out fell the papers from Box 1 – she was sure that a pattern would emerge. Undaunted, Amazonian, almost as convincing as convinced, she covered the floor with papers, worked with a belief in belief.

Now . . . Peter's paternal grandfather had discovered the mosaics at Bignor: 'So your father quite naturally took up history?'

'Naturally, yes.' The foot-binding quality of the family firm, the tradition that made RF and his son after him

43

subscribe to *Archaeology Today* rather than the *Pigeon Fancier*.

Nicola created a card-index system; she'd done much the same thing for her deep freeze. She questioned Peter about his father's life. School? Oxford? And as she did so, questions that he had failed to ask his father rained down upon him, thick and fast. 'Did you ever wish to do anything else? Did you feel you had a choice?' He remembered a story his father had told him about a faith healer he and Clem had met in Ireland after the Second World War. The healer was the seventh son of a seventh son who had been laying on of hands since the muscles in his arms had made him capable of the act. In answer to his father's question 'What would you have done if you hadn't been a seventh son?' he had said, all innocence and quite without irony, that he always fancied his chances on the stage . . . What would his father have done? Did the tracings suggest an artist? Did *The Journey from A* reveal a desire, a necessity, to write?

'Then he did Crete for his thesis and this was extended into his first and probably best-loved book.'

'Yes.'

'He went back and forth to Crete at least half a dozen times; he seems to have been in love with Crete.'

'He was.' Actually he wasn't, he was in love with Audrey, but he was married to her sister – life's rich tapestry, all that. Audrey was in that book, it was Audrey who had made it beautiful; she was in there, pressed between its pages like a flower.

'And then your mother died. Your father returned to Crete and after that moved about a bit; like your grandfather he was drawn to the Celtic Fringe.'

Peter gave this a guilty nod, described what he remembered of Angelsea and Hereford, South Wales, Cornwall and Penrith. Celtic Fringe my hat.

The morning passed. Nicola talked about words emerging like a medium seeing something forming in the vapours of a globe. 'Contribution is coming out,' she said, 'loud and clear. He was above all a contributor, wasn't he? How much of himself he put in . . .' And how little, Peter reflected, he took out.

Peter left her to it then, hovered uncertainly outside. Through the window he would see the angle of her bent and busy head, nice hair caught back. Close his eyes a little and he saw Kate's head, messier but equally marvelous to him. He remembered how the roles were then reversed: he would be in here working on *John Brown*, look up and see her drawing in the garden. 'When I look up . . .' Oh really! He used to watch her draw, think of her drawers, watch her draw, the first time they'd had a private conversation it had concerned pants. He in the sun room, Kate outside. How could she work when he could not, how dared she loll outside and draw? He watched her draw, he peered through the Venetian blinds, he envied her unselfconscious, happy absorption in her task. So he watched her, not what she drew but how she did it. When he tried to draw, he gripped the pencil in his fingers, pushed it like icing through a forcing bag; her drawing was by contrast flowing and continuous, although she was obviously more often than not dissatisfied with the result. She would hitch back her hair, gnaw at the end of her pencil, scratch her leg, roll the bracelets up and down her arm: 'And I have known the arms already, known them all, arms that are braceleted and white and bare but in the lamplight downed with light brown hair.' They were! They were! She rubbed at the absorbent paper with her fingers, smudging the lines. He couldn't help but admire, but of course he didn't say so; there was so much he didn't say then that he regretted now. It was courageous, he thought, this drawing onto blank paper. Like Nicola today, he never wrote a word without having done all the possible research, without that habitual thoroughness of approach. Time in reconnaissance, the walking man, pedestrian. They had a different approach to working, they talked about it once: an argument with all the important elements left out, whipping each other with theory as if it were barbed wire.

Kate, Kate. There were various things in Peter's life that he was ashamed of. The Salad King review and *Old John Brown* itself, the appeals of his father written on that typewriter from the sun room that he had chosen to ignore, the essentially messy affair with the Belgian poetess. These things shamed him but 'The Kate Business' – that's how he referred to it now – not only shamed him but filled him with regret, regret and a sort of fear for his own safety, his own survival, that he could have put a name to had he dared.

He could alter this or that to improve the scenario, an intelligent man can justify almost anything, and the justification went like this: his reluctance with Kate, his unnatural hesitation to dive in, splash about a bit, get wet, was not, in the context, his fault; blame could be laid elsewhere. It stemmed from Kate's connection with his family and, after all, the last thing one wished to do was play ball. The most significant thing about Kate Whittaker was that she had been, and still remained, very much a family friend.

A family affair. The Fox connection with the Whittakers was unlikely and long-winded. Richard Francis Fox, *this way blame*. Miss Poppleberg of Minnesota, Miss L. Poppleberg, 'Lindy' or 'Poppy' to her friends, was in charge of research at some nickel and dime university in the States, her subject 'Do parrots talk?' – in her terminology, 'A study into the vocalisation patterns of the African Grey'. Peter's father corresponded with Miss Poppleberg, a correspondence that had grown up from a Radio 3 concert-interval talk that had mentioned her research. The parrots had caught RF's interest and the ensuing correspondence, so far outside the natural habitat of his working life, refreshed and amused the old man and, in the last years's of his life, proved ironically to be quite a support. Through 'Poppy' another unlikely liaison had grown up. RF also corresponded with one Harold Whittaker in Guildford who kept his parrot, Archie, under the controlled test conditions that Miss Poppleberg applied to her caged birds. And through Whittaker RF had met his daughter, Kate.

'RF was such a walker!'

'Kate was such a dear!'

The friendship between RF in his late seventies and Kate,

blooming, all of twenty-five, was from the first a firm one. RF, 'so brilliant with students, with the young', was more interested in Kate than Archie, quick to see that Harold was more interested in Archie than in Kate. Under the protective wing went Kate. Kate had a wobbly fine-art career; RF commissioned a *Richard III* from her to grace the walls of his society, and when this painting received the anticipated 'mixed' reception (Kate's large, loud canvasses proved then and later on to be rather an acquired taste), he shared the joke with her. Kate became a protégée, a favourite. RF was revitalised by her and was quick to bestow the highest accolade of all: a visit to Cornwall to meet Audrey, down in Newlyn by the sea.

Neither Richard's taste in women nor the problems he encountered when dealing with them had changed much over the years. With Kate in tow he could face Audrey, but not for very long. He brought the two women together and then left them to it, and, as he had anticipated, they got on rather well. The sight of the two of them together in that poky seaside cottage pleased him as a tableau would; he liked the picture that they made and held it in his memory for a long, long time. Actually, for some reason, and he quite definitely did not wish to know what it was, Audrey seemed to have had a sobering effect on the young and bouncy Kate. The portrait that Kate made from sketches drawn on that day was more naturalistic than either of them expected. Richard paid for the finished portrait and sent it down to Audrey by Red Star. Audrey wrote to thank him for it but her letter, beginning in peace and ending in the usual recriminations, went unacknowledged by him. Over the next few years Kate visited Audrey on and off, but Richard, like his son after him, found reasons not to go. The correspondence with Audrey that had spanned more than a quarter of a century, that had begun and ended with a passion he did not like and cared not to understand, dwindled and finally dried up.

If Audrey gave no indication of being battle-weary, Richard her old lover had had more than enough. He did, however, continue to help Kate. He arranged a meeting with

Felix Switzer who ran a gallery in Cork Street, and patiently nursed this relationship until it eventually resulted in a successful London exhibition for his protégée, plus a commission or two on the side. Whether Richard or Felix really believed in Kate's talent, or whether both of them simply and instinctively believed in Kate, was immaterial to the outcome of those years. Kate had confidence, Kate believed in Kate, and it was Richard Fox she had to thank. Her father Harold had been edged out of the picture, in which RF now filled the frame. When Richard and Kate met up she would pester him about Audrey but he remained firm. In those last years of his life Richard did everything in his power for Kate – but he did not see Audrey again.

Peter might have met Kate at his father's funeral, had not Joyce's efficiency, even under strain, resulted in no woman but herself standing vigil at the grave. Thanks to her, neither Kate nor Audrey graced the dreadful day, but six weeks later, in May 1983, when spring began to blossom about The Round House whether its occupants were up to it or not, Ralph took himself off to Spain to 'get over things' and Kate accepted the offer of his cottage whilst he was away.

Peter did not espouse the conspiracy theory as Joyce did, but in the context of Kate and Ralph's offer he was never quite so sure. For once in his life Ralph had arranged things rather well. The idea – to get Kate into The Round House through the back door, and subsequently to get Audrey back there too – almost, but not quite, came off.

5

Peter had been proof-reading in the sun room, looking up and out through the French windows – pensive, no adrenalin flowing to protect him from the shock – when Kate walked confidently into the garden along Ralph's track, better looking than Ralph, younger, female, unknown, new.

The atmosphere that first day when she had joined them, uninvited, for morning coffee in the conservatory was decidedly chill. Her connection with Audrey put Joyce on the defensive. This, coupled with the fact that Peter had failed to insist that Kate and/or Audrey were informed directly of RF's death, considerably embarrassed them both. Should sides be the order of the day, then Peter, sitting there so comfortably with Joyce, had chosen the wrong one. Kate had a lot to thank RF for and she recognised the debt. She now lived and worked at Felix Switzer's studio in the Tottenham Court Road and Felix had exhibited her in Cork Street, and would do so again. Broke at the beginning of '83, she had wavered between taking up a bursary or trying to get a job. Felix's vested interest suggested the bursary; RF had plumped for the job. As usual, Kate had taken the older man's advice.

Peter had avoided meeting Kate before – *the last thing one wished to do was play ball*. Refusing his father's invitation to Kate's opening view, he had followed the exhibition in the papers: 'Brooding and chaotic with colour' – *Financial Times*; 'Narratives of a threateningly ambivalent style' – Waldemar Januszczak in the *Guardian*. Intrigued, Peter had gone off on his own one afternoon to see what there was to see for himself. He didn't like it – well, he didn't understand it – but one picture had him rooted to the spot. *Daring Miss*

Pears, a huge black and red canvas which on close inspection revealed its narrative: a child eating bluebells with a wolf/angel at her side. He'd looked at it for a long time but moved off quickly when someone who might/might not be Felix had glided towards him with intent. He actually wanted to meet her from this point, though he had made no attempt to do so; now, here she was, sitting at the table with them both, telling them, whether they were interested or not, all about her job.

Blackbird, the children's educational publishers, had commissioned Kate to revitalise a series of early reading books. Blackbird, so meek and so mild; Kate Whittaker, chaotic with colour: Peter almost fell from his chair with shock. Kate could explain it all. She insisted that she'd got the job because she was so fat, but she wasn't fat, not really, large, ample, hardly massive, but she spoke of herself in Hattie Jacques's terms, as fat. For firms like Blackbird, she said, the body made a greater impression than the talent or the mind. Fashions impinge, and firms like Blackbird believe, as Julius Caesar did, that the fat ones are okay. (This wasn't quite what Shakespeare had said on behalf of Caesar but, like much else with Kate, Peter let it pass.) According to her, there was something reassuring about fat, perhaps its folds, that made even the most unstable person appear reliable and good. In Blackbird's eyes, unreliable artists, characters who failed to meet deadlines or propositioned senior members of staff, were wraith-like Trots with suspicious coughs; the best of them actually spat blood.

Kate's present task, which she had begun that very morning over in Ralph's kitchenette, was to turn her hand to Janet and Jim, the little figures who iced the rock-hard bun of early reading books. Apparently – and this was new to Joyce and Peter obviously, so she would explain – fashions in reading, phonetics, 'Look and See', come and go, but Janet and Jim with their staccato cries of 'I like the ball'/'Pat likes the ball'/'I like Pat' had withstood the test of time. Quick readers raced at them, reluctant readers struggled manfully through, teachers ('and aren't teachers awfully like orienteers?') trusted this slowly assimilated controlled vocabulary.

Janet and Jim were solid gold, built to run and run. However, and this seemed at last to be the point – Kate flapped her hands expressively, Peter noticed the hands – if reading had changed little, fashions had changed a lot and the Aertex look of Janet and Jim, that unavoidably English middle-class sense of Chilprufe vests and full employment, of white-is-wonderful and mummy-bakes-a-cake, had recently come under scrutiny at the office. The text might stand, but Janet and Jim, though saying the same old things and remaining sure of leg and limb (you know the type of children who *automatically* wash their hands after going to the loo), had to be revamped. The illustrations must be updated. Janet and Jim must get out of Viyella and into the sort of velour jogging suits – 'Grim, I know, – now cheaply available to all. According to a middle-class member of the board, the children were divisively middle-class. This distinction stretched beyond clothes to include the outside world. How? Well, obviously they would stop going to the butcher/baker and be seen standing at the check-out in the queue. Jim, in response to feminist ideas, which Blackbird could no longer afford to overlook, might now be seen helping mummy with the washing-up, Janet handing hammer and nails to daddy as he built the rabbit hutch.

Joyce was mildly diverted by this speech, although at pains not to show it; Peter, despite himself, was positively intrigued. During the telling of her story, he had first been jealous of his father, then of Felix, and now, quite definitely, of the middle-class member of the board. Seeing Kate was like suddenly remembering the existence of good music; it reminded him that he was miserable, lonely and considerably bored; no one could have described the girl as fat. Still, the Audrey connection, his mother's sister, was a painful one to him, and more pertinent still was the fact that Kate had been his father's girl. *Ever yours, Newlyn '78 . . .*

For these reasons he did not pursue her but concentrated his mind on *Old John Brown*, a concentration which in the event proved to be a little flawed. He hoped she would disturb him and was disturbed when she did not. After a day or two of being irritatingly left in peace John Brown was discarded in favour of Ig, whose already well-read auto-biography Peter took out into the garden to read. The delightful possibility of friendship with this girl was worth the rage he felt when leafing through this book; the means might justify the end, so he settled himself in the Lloyd loom chair with the footrest, a pencil ready in his hand. The thought of systematically defacing Ig's book appealed to Peter. He relaxed in the ancient chair, comfortable but rather cold, only partly sheltered in the lee of the bamboo hedge. Due to his close proximity to Ralph's cottage, his position – one might call it 'strategic' – virtually across Ralph's path, it was not altogether surprising that Kate and Peter met that afternon, met and met again. Peter was disturbed from Ig's opinionated voice by Kate: 'Have you seen my pants?' Was this an invitation? 'They flew off the line.'

'Blew.'

'No, red . . .'

He denied all knowledge of these pants, though he had in fact spotted them only minutes before. Reading an exceptionally boring passage – Ig holding forth on the camber of Roman roads – his mind had wandered, his eye been diverted, caught by an unusual colour in the garden, a patch of red which, on closer inspection, had revealed itself as Satin Kayser Caminicks and sent him scurrying back to Rome.

'Mind if I scout around?'

'By all means.'

She moved off and a few seconds later 'Got them!' she said, coming back to him, waving them aloft like some terrible flag. 'Honestly, Peter, they must have been right under your nose.'

Perish the thought, oh wondrous thought.

Embarrassed, he had merely smiled and withdrawn, enigmatically he hoped, into his book. But he was keen, he couldn't help himself; his interest had been kindled and the pants had fanned the flame of the growing fire, of that there could not now be any reasonable doubt.

He watched her trail off for a walk. Ig seemed, if possible, more pompous, the air quite definitely damp. Patiently he waited for her return. And yes, here she came. She sat down, quite uninvited, on the grass beyond his chair and asked him, quite without hesitation, what he was *still* doing.

'I'm reading this book.' He flapped the cover for her to see: Ig in a Barbour standing over a hole.

'Good?'

'I have read it before.'

'Must be good.'

'It's interesting. It refers,' a dip in his voice, it did seem silly, 'to my father.'

'Oh.' She yawned and lay back on the damp grass, he wondered idly about the colour of her pants. 'I do miss him,' she said. 'You are lucky. I can't imagine my father ever being mentioned in a book.'

'Miss Poppleberg might mention him?'

'Oh, you know about Poppy, do you?'

'Of course.'

'Well, I doubt if Archie really makes the grade,' she said. 'In weak moments I wish my father had been a burglar or a car salesman. Banking's a joke, isn't it; whatever way you turn the thing, it's dull. I mean, one is tempted to reinvent oneself, don't you think?'

'I hadn't considered it,' Peter lied.

'I do all the time,' Kate said – she was a chatterbox, as lively as Peter felt himself to be flat. 'My father's retired now but it doesn't really help.'

'Really?'

'He spends most of his time with Archie or in the garden. I thought he might do something more interesting now. I told him, now's your chance.' She looked glum. 'He's not interested in anything interesting, that's the thing. Then there's the body blow, you heard about that?'

'No.'

'My brother's in prison in America for drugs.'

'Oh dear.'

'Yes, it is "Oh dear". It was all over the *Daily Express*. I don't mind. Obviously I'm really sorry it happened, sorry he was caught – the *Express* is what gets them of course. My mother says he'll never get over it.'

'Your father or your brother?'

'Most definitely dad. David's all right, he's doing a business studies' course, learning to type and compute and everything.'

'I see.'

She got up, stretched. 'Why don't you come over later on, to Ralph's, have a drink or something? I can't stick it out here any longer. Why is it so bloody windy and cold?'

And he had done. He'd brushed his teeth, slipped out and along Ralph's path. He watched her draw, saw her, spoke to her once, twice, every day. The weather got worse, colder, wetter, windier; rainbows hung from every tree. The oh-so-casual friendly neighbour, he would wander across like a moth to the light at Ralph's kitchen door.

'How's it going?'

'Ugh.'

'Already?'

'A bit dull, not yet deadly.'

'Oh dear.'

Kate worked from early morning to early afternoon, then, in the evening, among the night life of that dripping kitchen – woodlice, silverfish, daddy-longlegs, spiders, moths – looked at it again.

'Felix works the other way round,' she told him. 'Sometimes he stays up half the night.'

Peter hated Felix, he did not wish to know. 'How are the little monsters?' he would ask of Janet and Jim.

'In rude health – not very rude, in dull health.' She'd lift the sheet of tissue which covered the work in progress. 'Here.' Her hair would fall forward as she bent. 'Here.'

'What are they doing?'

'Putting something into the trolley.'

'Glue?'

'Cereal, I thought.'

Peter stuck to glue. Despite the change of costume, the children remained essentially the same, there was something instinctively 'goody-goody' about them both. He suggested all sorts of plans that might alter this, and she, who wanted children of her own rather desperately since David had gone to prison, since RF had died, thought how odd it was – she and Peter, replacing the tissue over the illustration – discussing the children after they had gone to bed.

But Peter was exhilarated by Kate; it was virtually impossible to disguise. He leant, legs crossed at the ankles, arms folded, against Ralph's sweaty, oddly buzzing fridge. Kate turned and twisted on the piano stool she had found from somewhere, wound up to its maximum, the table by the sash window, the window frame rotten with damp and moss.

'Make it glue,' he said, 'And then they sneak out without paying. There's a packet of Smarties in Janet's pocket, Jim has already eaten a Lion Bar and has two more up his sleeve. Where's Daddy? He ought to be in there somewhere with the list?'

'He's in the park sailing a boat.' She leant up and across to the shelf above her head where Ralph's soggy individual-sized mustards and curry powders had been pushed to one side to make way for her copies of previous Blackbird editions.

'He looks furtive,' Peter said of Daddy. 'Off to collect his dole?'

'Dole is sent to you these days.'

'Is it? Oh. Well, it doesn't arrive and he bites the postman.'

Kate yawned and yawned because the country air, the work, was tiring. She turned the little pages. 'Then they take the bus to London Zoo, where the children are particularly interested in the pandas.'

'Why pandas?'

'Pandas is an easy word, anyway I'm good at pandas.' She smiled, her smiles a knife through butter.

Peter frowned. 'Before they can reach the panda cage a rogue elephant eats them up.'

'They couldn't cope with "rogue" – anyway, they can't be eaten up, we're only on Stage 1. They haven't got the vocabulary, you see; rogue's quite difficult if you think about it.' She thought he looked rather disappointed. 'You ought to write fiction,' she suggested.

'I don't think so.'

'Why not?'

'What does the father do?' he said, now avoiding this difficult tack. 'He's an estate agent, or he works for the waterboard . . . What does he do at weekends?'

'He's very busy, a handyman. Making the rabbit hutch, sailing the model boat, he does a lot of things in the garage.' She giggled. 'Here: "Daddy goes to work in the garage" – it's a bit misleading really. I've never taught anyone to read.' She yawned and got down from the piano stool, began to rinse the cups and brushes under the running tap. It was the signal for him to go.

'While in the reptile house . . .'

'By the panda cage.'

'The pandas are being strangled to death by a mad keeper, who . . .'

'Too exciting,' she said firmly.

He watched her, too exciting. He wanted to leave and he wanted to stay. He wanted to go back to the comparative safety of the sun room, he wanted to curl himself up and sleep in his own armchair; he wanted to sleep here with her.

'There is one thing,' she said as he was leaving.

'What?'

She picked up the book and held the relevant page up to the light. He came and stood beside her, quite close. 'Jim's ball gets stuck in a tree.'

'Balls?'

'Ball.'

Those evenings, Peter returned, still in the light, along Ralph's path to the house. Joyce asleep with an eye-shade RF had got her on a trip out to Hong Kong, he sat in his bedroom, moody in the armchair. Here he tried out conversations for Kate; for someone of his fluency, the apt and larval phrase, these conversations stuttered out of him, English as a foreign language for those who cannot cope with

56

love: 'As it's rained most of the time, you probably won't want to return. I expect you find the country rather dull after living in London. It's a pity you didn't see the place in the sunshine – *it's lovely here in autumn, do come down* – it has been a pity about the wind. If you did decide to come back again, it would probably be better if you worked over here. Ralph has never been away before and is unlikely to make a habit of it. Joyce's old office or the scullery could easily be turned into a studio for you. I've had a look at the scullery and it seems, even in this gloom, to get a decent light. I shall be terribly busy of course. I shall probably soon start on another book. If you really wanted to visit Audrey, we could go together, make a day of it, I shouldn't mind at all. I gather from Ralph that lately she's been rather frail . . .'

What was Kate's generation? He had missed it in all those years of writing about the past. Should he say, 'I believe there's a discotheque in the town'? Was there? He had no idea. He tried to imagine himself dancing, one two three, one two three.

One late afternoon he walked across to Ralph's carrying this invitation to her much as Ralph walked the other way with the *Telegraph* under his arm. It had been raining but the sun was coming out now; unfortunately she did not appear to be about. The door was shut, he peered through the open window of the built-on bathroom; on the cistern of the loo a horrifying bumper box of Tampax met his eye. He called through the window.

'Washing my hair,' came Kate's voice from upstairs.

'Oh.'

'Put the kettle on if you like.'

'Rightio.' What was he saying now? He never said 'Rightio'.

Now the sun streamed through the kitchen door onto the stoop; he made a pot of teabag tea in china already sticky, tanin-brown by use. She came out to join him, her head wrapped enormous in a frayed and greying towel.

When you go, he thought, I'll never wash my hair, I'll never brush my teeth, I'll let both fall out as proof. He'd begun to read poetry again, he couldn't help himself, Stevie Smith and Charlotte Mew. Kate, Kate, he was seriously disturbed by Kate – but he didn't mention the disco, they talked of other things, didn't invite her to the dance or try to stop her leaving, didn't try anything at all.

I'd like to tell you . . . you may not be aware that . . . what I mean to say is . . . that I'm really enjoying this cup of tea. This cup of tea on this stoop is all I really want, what I want, and I want to stretch it out, make it last a little while. I want to be absorbed in you and drinking tea, like this together, I wanted you to know, to allow me this tea with you . . .

And Kate thought that Peter was terribly reserved, most peculiar, not like his father, not a bit. He hung about but nothing happened, he hadn't even asked her to go out for a drink.

6

Back in the sun room a definite policy was pursued. The set of Nicola's Alice band, the determination of that chin, assured him that it was policy, not simply chaos or mess. Like the government of the day, she explained that things had to get worse before they got better. Peter, demoted, joined the ranks of the lifeless, the unemployed.

The boxfiles, empty, were stacked on the divan; a process of piling rather than filing took shape on the floor. Peter actually had to step gingerly through his father's life in order to cross to the long table by the wall that now served as his desk.

'No wonder you couldn't see the wood for the trees,' said Nicola, to whom Peter had said no such thing. 'I've put a pile of herrings on your desk if you want to go through them.'

'Thanks.'

'Bills, that sort of thing.'

'Fine.'

'Oh, and Eric Bloodaxe is in the wall cupboard; I thought I ought to keep that separate for a bit. It could make a paper at least, there's quite a lot of it, all good stuff. I don't know what you think?'

'Nor do I.'

'Sorry?' Nicola's gold lighter snip-snapped open; did it sound irritated? Peter rather thought it did.

'Whatever you think,' he said.

'Well do have a look at it, won't you.'

'Of course.'

Life with Nicola was rather like marriage. Peter felt like the earnest, DIY father of Kate's Janet and Jim: 'Could you look at the hoover for me, darling, it doesn't seem to be picking up. Something awful seems to have happened to the iron . . .' Peter rankled at the thought that he was now being given simple, unimportant tasks to keep him occupied, the whingeing pre-school child given the colour supplement and a pair of specially blunt scissors: 'Why don't you do a bit of cutting-out before lunch?'

Peter occupied himself with his pile. Bills, most of them, went into the waste basket; there were a lot of bills. In his last years his father had occupied himself with the hoover side of life that Peter had previously assumed to be the role of Joyce. The boiler, deliveries of coal and coke, when the chimneys were swept, orders for logs, car tax and MOT, insurance, Ralph's cottage: domesticity shot through with defiance, his father keeping his head above water, but only just. On the reverse of a bill from Butler Oils he had written: *We live in the age of fast travel, planes, boats, trains, hovercraft, shuttles, skateboards. Even here, I must believe it, pizzas can be delivered to my door.* But if his father felt trapped by domesticity, he still held firm to the possibility of escape. Here were plans to move and how much it would cost him; details of a two-up two-down keeper's cottage on the Murgadale estate; details from the Admiralty on the proposed sale of Calshot Spit lifeboat – in sight of the Isle of Wight? Here the deliciously ironic season swimming ticket, unstamped; brochures from the 1982 Boat Show at Earls Court. Running parallel to this were examples of how much was still expected of Richard Francis, into his eighties and on. Books by other historians sent by publishers for the ubiquitous glowing quote. 'So what?' he found written on a compliments slip from Cape. Letters from students, invitations to digs and exhibitions – *What is all this clap trap about India*? – lectures, after-dinner speeches, presentations of awards. Comments scribbled on the back of these revealed a weary and depressed old man.

Because his father hadn't published anything in the last years of his life, these years were considered to be herring years and consequently were being written off. The half-cock projects, the correspondence with Miss Poppleberg, the friendship with Kate – all this being discarded because it failed sufficiently to add up. Women always made it their business to try and alter men, thought Peter, observing Nicola at her work; it must be vanity or something, the unerring sense that they know what is best. Nicola discarded this, made more of that, handed him over more 'stuff'. She was making the man presentable again, arranging his face to meet the press again: on Peter's desk were tales of disappointment, defeat, depression, disillusion and dismay; at Nicola's desk by the window 'energy' and 'contribution' were running neck and neck.

'Can you make anything of this lot? What do you think of this?' Another sheaf of papers came across; for Peter the biographer, his art seemed suddenly to pass beyond the pale. If it doesn't add up, it has to be left out; find a peg to hang it on, or else – how often had he made much the same bleak progresses himself? The man who'd written *The Journey from A* was now trimmed to fit snugly, cosily, under headings B, C, D, E and F, possibly even G. Nicola's fine Edding Profipen spread across the life that, it now occurred to Peter, had been quite different from the already accepted myth. Only connect, he thought. My God, what a dangerous and ultimately deceitful game. Nicola's pen made loops and footbridges, constructed the overpass, re-routed the one-way street; opening up the cul-de-sac, overruling the signs: *This way blame*, 'Welcome to the Isle of Wight', 'Dead End'.

The Victorian porch had been erected because at that time it had been useful to have somewhere to hang the coats, but Nicola would have nothing to do with an edifice of that sort. When the book came out, the writing would be in a straight line without spaces; there would be chapters and full stops and new paragraphs and captioned pictures and footnotes, indexes, bibliography – biography, order out of chaos, quite suddenly anathema to him.

Perhaps the size of the herring pile was more significant than the motley he knew it to contain. Would he put it to her, before it was too late, that the herrings made up the man?

61

Perhaps there was pride to be won in Hayward's at the time so beastly and destructive words 'Ho Ho' attached to the Salad King review. Something to be made from the old chestnut that history was fiction after all, that passion and philosophy, while being the twin enemies of history, were also qualities quite natural to man. A concentration on herrings led to a general dissembling, but biography without it was pure puff. *Must get Clem off my back* – well, his father had been a failure as much as a success, a paragon and a pig. Nicola was well intentioned, she made the sun room bearable for him; would he allow her to exorcise the ghost?

Is this the father whose feet I used to dance on squashed flat between the covers of a book? I'm looking for my father? Right here, sir, in this urn. Is this it, all of it, it looks so uniform and small, I hardly recognise the man at all.'

He recalled an argument with Kate on her last morning at Ralph's cottage. He leant back in his chair, irritating Nicola as much as if he had undressed and tucked himself prone on the divan, thought back to that day in May 1983: their first argument, their first sparring match, the difference of opinion that struck home.

Ostensibly it had been an argument about painting *v.* writing – hardly a comparison of like with like. Underlying it was an argument in which Peter said 'stay' and Kate said 'I'm going', and to Kate, who leapt to all sorts of ill-considered conclusions, it turned quite simply on the matter of life and death. She was on the side of life; Peter, as Audrey had said of his father, represented death.

'I know I'd loathe it,' Kate said about writing. 'I don't know how you do it, it wouldn't do for me.' She wanted to be unkind to him, she wanted to make some distance; they sat in Ralph's kitchen drinking coffee and systematically, well systematically for her, she disparaged what he was and what he did.

'Biography especially, all that beginning with birth and ending in death, it's so inexorable, doom, doom, always working towards an end.'

'You work towards an end, in your painting, surely . . .'

'I don't, well only vaguely.' He looked grumpy, she felt cross; neither of them liked the day or what it meant to both of them, neither liked the prospect of goodbye. 'I don't work towards an end,' she insisted. 'It's a different thing entirely, full of surprises and disappointments, whereas you . . . in those fine, clean lines you so admire, end up robbed of both.'

'Explain.'

'I will. I have a picture in my mind which I work towards but in the execution of it the picture often becomes, well in some ways always becomes, something else. Can you understand that?'

'I think so.'

'Because of the way I work, live, my end product is always something of a surprise. I like surprises,' she stated, implying that he did not. 'I'm not frightened of surprises,' she lied, for Peter was a surprise to her, a substantial one. 'I suppose that's why I always wonder, did I really do that, it's unexpected. What you do is predictable, predictable and dull.'

'Not necessarily dull.'

'And you are fully aware of every plodding step. Off you go, Peter Fox, eight books on, marching determinedly from beginning to end in a very straight, unwavering, beastly line.'

'Now you're making the whole thing sound blinkered.'

'It is blinkered, that's the point.'

What had his father said? People are trapped in history and history is trapped in them. Had he wound himself up totally, double-trapped himself in solid, blinkered books? Ralph would turn up any minute, there was precious little time, he had to say what he had come to say: 'Stay'. They jockeyed for position; it was a silly, ill-based argument but neither could bear it if the other won. 'Okay,' he said, instead of 'Stay', 'but to me your approach is undisciplined, time-consuming and probably extremely frustrating.'

'It isn't.'

'You have an idea of what to go for and you end up with something else; that seems to carry an element of frustration to me. You're like the free man who ends up with a wife, two children, a mortgage, a car to clean and polish and an annual holiday in Spain, who cries, "This is what I've always wanted." '

'The point is' – she loved and hated him, he would not move – 'that what I get in the end might actually be what I really meant at the beginning, might be what I wanted in the first place, might be something even better.'

'Might. Having got there, you pretend. If this vision of yours was ever clear in the first place, you would work for it, and each time you found it being impinged upon, interfered with, you'd protest –'

'But life isn't like that!' she protested.

'It could be, if you wanted it to be.'

'No thanks.'

'You could rub out, paint over, or whatever it is you do, and you'd end up with the vision you began with.'

'Allelulia! And look what I might lose. I've got to be open to all eventualities, possibilities.'

'And risk ending up with nothing.'

'Yes absolutely.' God how she hated him. 'Risk.'

The word sunk in. 'It all sounds pretentious to me,' said Peter.

'It would, to you. There's something wrong with you, you daren't dare. Can't you do that? I can't understand you, what is the matter, we're different people. I just don't understand you at all . . . If I didn't meander, I would lose my way. Does that make any sense to you at all? I'd miss everybody, everything. When I'm working, opportunities present themselves, I'm lured.'

'We're all lured but it doesn't mean necessarily that we follow.'

'Head over heart, congratulations. Anyway I think you're lying. You're not lured, you're too pompous, you're not lured in anything you do or say. I see no evidence of it at all. You're not blinkered, you're blind. A blind creator of straight lines.' She paused for breath. 'You're nothing like your father; you're a presser and an ironer, and you're trapped. Life is full of bulges which you make it your business to iron out, you

64

flatten and you press. History is fiction, biography is fiction, and it frightens you to death. All the causes of wars, Archduke Ferdinand, all that gunk, because it's retrospective and written by pompous people like you, it's fictional –'

'It's fact.'

'You can't convince me. I don't believe a word you say.' (I'm going home.) 'No matter how much you try to avoid it, you must take, because you are you, an angle on something, a point of view. You are like me but you daren't say so. What you write is particular because it's you that writes it; like history, it's subjective, your vision, however much you disown it.' She thought of his solid biographies that his father had found so worrying, so mean and thin. He'll never leave this house, she thought, he pretends to hate it but it suits him rather well. He bends things and makes them into straight lines. I'd be a fool to let him get his hands on me.

'We'll have to agree to disagree,' he suggested.

'I never do that,' she said.

Ralph's single postcard from Spain, a toreador, had arrived that day, the same day as Ralph himself did. There was a conflab in the cottage after Peter left, Ralph trying to persuade Kate to stay. Ralph, with confidence boosted by time away and a slight tan, trying to get through to Kate. He hadn't been away for years and more than the weather seemed cold to him when he returned. That trick of the light that makes the possibility of changing things suddenly less remote affected him as his plane had made the approach to Gatwick, so that by the time he eventually made it back to his own cottage door the old sterility of life at The Round House, Joyce and Peter and the ghost of his friend RF were briefly but vividly clear. Kate ought to stay, it would enrich their lives. In mounting consternation about the state of his own life – the stark contrast with the Ralph on the beach on the sunny holiday abroad – it seemed to him that Kate represented the last chance, last runner, the one that he should back. 'Say you'll stay,' he urged her, 'at least until your commission is complete,' but Kate had already made up her mind to go. She had used the argument with Peter earlier that morning to shore herself up against the wave of him, against what had come over her in those two weeks at Ralph's cottage, the sea change that would change the pattern of her life if she let it. Like Audrey before her, there was something about The Round House that simultaneously attracted and repelled her. Audrey's life was an unhappy one and Kate was very young; she wouldn't move in anywhere with anyone who represented death.

7

If Ralph felt momentarily abandoned when Kate left, Peter, lucid now that she was out of earshot, was 'broken and bereft'. For him 1983 was a long and sterile summer. *John Brown* had gone to his publisher and, the trickle of romantics to the shrine apart, a quiet descended on The Round House which was indeed very much like death.

Without Kate to distract him his obsession with her grew; he imagined them together in a different world where the grass was greener and there wasn't any past. He saw them in a garden, quiet in deckchairs, in a garden looking out. Kate had been a chatterbox; in his vision she became serene and quiet. Kate and him quietly sitting, Kate and Peter quiet, Kate as a hedge against a horrid life, Kate as a shelter and a lap, Kate, a nursing nun perhaps, Kate as a pool of quiet. Without her Ralph seemed more hopeless, Joyce more intransigent, his father's ghost impossible to usurp. The Round House was all corners without Kate, the peace of the long dull summer days incapable of quiet.

But there was to be no quiet for Peter, and in early September peace was shattered too. Audrey, travelling for some unknown reason between the historic towns of Glastonbury and Wells, had been taken ill on a National Coach and admitted to a private nursing home not forty miles away. Coffee was late on the day of matron's sudden call.

Audrey ill, not dead: the news for Joyce could hardly have been worse. She was furious, she couldn't bear it, although she knew she must. Down in the kitchen, the top of the marmalade flew from her hands and rolled wilfully away beneath the settle and far out of her grasp.

'RF was such a walker.'

'Audrey was always a perfect bitch.'

A pan lid got away from her, fell and clattered on the sloping floor. Joyce was in charge now and she would not have that woman in the house. Audrey ill, absolutely typical, and not forty miles away. A convalescent Audrey, a nightmare – the process would be long, drawn out, be slow: this was something Joyce could well do without. Joyce, who had loved RF as much as Audrey had ever done . . . The fact that her love, like Audrey's, had never made either of them happy, that Audrey's life had been, apart from those months in Crete, as unhappy and as unfulfilled as her own, did not occur to Joyce in that early morning agony in the kitchen. Audrey had always been, would always be, a fish hook embedded in the flesh. The fact that she still stalked the earth, albeit with unflattering elephantiasis of the ankles and the aid of a very stout stick, had never been far from Joyce's frail and guilty consciousness. Age had got Audrey by the ankles, Joyce by the elbows and wrists – but, should they both have been reduced to torsos, they would have fought it out. Now Audrey ill, ill close by, how typical of the woman! There was bound to be a really ghastly fuss. Joyce scraped at her arms with her fingernails, thinking of Audrey's face, and bypassed God to appeal now to Nesta in her hour of need. It was Nesta who'd told her to tell Clem about Audrey, and Joyce had always grudgingly done what Nesta had advised. Audrey made an art of putting people in difficult positions. It was Audrey who'd put the idea into RF's head that Joyce was 'interfering'; she'd only done what Nesta had told her she 'ought' to do – God was deaf, it really was too bad. A fuss was unavoidable now; everything so neatly folded, so near to being forgotten, would be turned out of the closet once again. Ralph was fond of Audrey, Audrey was Peter's only surviving aunt, and Joyce hated her: she would not have that woman in her house. All this went through Joyce's mind as she prepared the coffee on the day that news about Audrey began to filter through.

'We'll have to go and see her.' Ralph was insistent. 'Someone ought to go today.'

'It would be pointless to go today. She's hardly *compos mentis* at the moment, Ralph. It would be silly to drive all that way –'

'She'll have to come back here.'

'That's out of the question. In any case, she's probably far too ill.'

'You said matron said a very minor stroke. You'll have to have her here.'

'Don't tell me what I have to do, Ralph, please.'

Joyce drank her coffee, her hands shook. All her instincts were to shriek 'No! No!', to say 'absolutely, categorically not', to thump the conservatory table until the blue cups jumped. 'I can't possibly care properly for her here,' she said, mustering considerable reserve.

'But –'

'No buts, Ralph. I'm sorry. It simply can't be done. This house is quite impossible for an invalid, we'd have to get a nurse, we can't afford a nurse. How would Audrey manage? She couldn't even tackle the stairs.'

'We could put her in the drawing room.'

'No! No!' Joyce scrabbled at her arm. 'She can't possibly travel, anywhere, not at the moment. It would be impossible in this house. Think back a bit, remember how difficult it was with Clem?'

A moment's silence followed this remark. Joyce had gone a bit too far. No one over mentioned, cared to remember, how difficult it was with Clem.

'But if she's dying –' Ralph ventured.

'She isn't dying. Who said anything about her dying! Audrey has had a minor stroke, she isn't dying. Really, Ralph, I do think we can do without your histrionics at a time like this.'

'What exactly did matron say?'

'I told you! I have already told you what the matron said. Matron said that Audrey had suffered a very minor stroke.'

'I wish you'd called me to the phone.'

'I can cope with a phone call, Ralph!'

'Well,' Ralph stood up, the *Telegraph* unopened, the coffee hardly even touched, 'I shall go and have a word with Peter.'

'You can't. He's gone for a walk.'

'You have told him, I hope?'

'Don't be sanctimonious with me, Ralph. Of course I told him, straight away.'

'I rather think you might have taken the trouble to come across and inform me.'

'I have informed you.'

Ralph hovered in the doorway, letting in the draught. His position was intolerable, he had no power; he would not, could not, let Joyce get away with this. 'I'll find Peter, I'll talk it over with him. I think we should ring back.'

'Ring back by all means, Ralph. No one is stopping you from using the phone.'

'I shall, and I'll go and visit her today whatever state she's in. Don't try and stop me, Joyce. I don't understand your attitude at all. I'll go and visit her today. Someone's got to show the flag.'

'Whatever you like, my dear.' She wished him luck with it. In case Ralph had overlooked it, Audrey was the type of woman who stamped on flags.

Peter was unhelpful. Ralph went on his own. It upset him dreadfully; driving there and back in Peter's car through the flying leaves, he returned exhausted, emotionally quite spent and shaky at the knees. 'Tragic,' he told Peter, winding down the window as he drove into the barn. 'Really very, very frail.'

'Did you check the oil, Ralph?'

'No.' Peter had asked him to check the oil but Ralph was in no state to remember things like that.

'But it went all right?'

'The car yes. The visit was not an unqualified success. She's paralysed, only slightly. She's suffering, you know, in a considerable amount of pain.'

Peter managed a nod of the head.

'You will go and see her, won't you. She did ask me.'

'Did you ask her to come here?' asked Peter, poking beneath the bonnet of the car.

Ralph raised his eyebrows to the sky. 'Nothing would possess her. Adamant refusal.' Ralph now cocked his head in the direction of the house. 'You know, not keen on old Joyce –'

'I gather the feeling's mutual.'

'Yes.' Ralph drew in breath dramatically. 'I'm afraid it is. It's all quite wrong, you know,' he said more firmly, 'ridiculous and stupid at this time of life. What's past is past. Audrey's nearly eighty and Joyce's what, sixty-four, -five?'

'Well –'

'More than "well" is called for, more than "well". At this stage of the game. Your father would turn in his grave if he knew anything of this.' Ralph was tired, exhausted, shattered. 'Ought to be able to put these things to one side, you know. Tragic,' he reproached Peter, who made a business of putting the oil can securely to one side.

'Are you coming into the house?'

'No, not this evening, not tonight.'

They left the car and walked towards Ralph's path. 'Kate's coming down,' he said. 'I phoned her from the hospital. Audrey asked for her. I didn't think you'd mind.'

'No, of course.' Peter digested this bit of information, he too felt suddenly shaky at the knees. 'Have you told Joyce?'

'Not exactly. I wondered if you might?'

'Of course. Now you get home to bed.'

Ralph caught his arm as he turned through the bamboo hedge. 'Come across if anything turns up, won't you,' he begged Peter. 'Keep me informed.'

'I will.'

'Tragic,' said Ralph for the umpteenth time, parting from Peter, tragically taking his path.

Ralph collected Kate at the station. She had tea with him at the cottage and then, as Ralph was anxious to avoid Joyce, made her way over to The Round House by herself. 'I'm not sure where Peter is,' Ralph said, 'but Joyce's about somewhere.'

'She is expecting me?'

'Oh yes. About somewhere,' Ralph said guiltily and darted back behind the safety of his hedge.

Kate too cursed Audrey's propinquity to The Round House. Looking at it now, she wished she hadn't come. She walked across to the front door, went in, pushed open the second door without excitement, did not call for Joyce but simply stood, alone there in the hall. Perhaps it was the autumn or the fact that during that long summer in London her imagination had somehow got the details wrong; it was only September, but she disliked the autumn and she knew she also disliked the house. Quite alone, she prowled about downstairs. Richard she had seen only in London and she had been no further than the conservatory during her stay at Ralph's; to her, the old house was quite new.

The layout, owing to it's circularity, was peculiar – old but not very attractive. One had to enter one room to get to another. The place that evening in September was heavy and dark and echoing, held the early autumn damp and cold. The hall ran the depth of the house. A Persian runner, no longer running straight, partially covered the flagstones, a window looked out to a beech copse at the back. A pretty half-moon table, letters on a silver salver, two addressed to Peter, she picked them up and looked at them. What have I, she wondered, got to do with this? Returning them to the salver, her eyes took in an empty copper jug with a pewter handle which caught the dull light from the window at the back. She surveyed it all, dispassionate observer, her heart still. As an artist she observed the delicacy of the legs of the half-moon table in the darkness and solidity of the house; how could something so fragile survive its overwhelming, heavy presence? She imagined the hostility of the old round walls to this table and its little legs, the walls fighting against the melting feminine table, glorying in the emptiness of the jug. She looked once more at the letters on the salver, his letters waiting for him in the old, dark, empty house. The dining room: eight chairs, two carvers, paintings of the dead in matching frames, Uncle Binks and Uncle Gooding, Grandmother and Grandfather Fox, dead people, glass eyes, observing her observing them. From this she went back into the hall – past the crocodile with the gong in its mouth, the umbrellas, golf clubs, walking sticks – through a baize-covered door into the kitchen, which one entered like a boat beneath the sea, clammy, an enormously high ceiling here, the wall broken by a dado rail at the height of a child and Peter had probably run his finger along this . . . She couldn't get into the sun room. There must be a knack of opening the door, easy when you know how; she hoped she wasn't there long enough to find out. Back to the kitchen and into the scullery, which immediately she liked. A whitewashed bright room that lifted her, which looked out to the downs and to a far-off clump of trees. Do I love him? Do I? Do I? Here she could rest and think. Joyce must be about somewhere, Kate deliberated, but she did not like to go upstairs. She waited, still no Joyce, still no Peter.

She wandered aimlessly in the house, homing back to the scullery, the sanctuary of the scullery again. Trapped puss moths in the corner of the glass, she looked out at the far-off clump of trees. How the wind must take them up in the winter, she thought. Their position, as she perceived her own that evening, was unenviably exposed. The old leaves would take up the rustle, one to the other, waves of sound. She liked the room, she'd like to paint it, paint in it – Peter? Turning away from the view, she took in the rest of it: the buzzing freezer, the washing machine with its small packet of washing powder, a measuring cup, some tongs. An inner hall and then, oh God, another window facing, like the one in the hall did, to the back. Here she studied the beech copse once again, imagined herself alone there just as she was alone here now in the house. She hated beeches as much as autumn, the beeches would be vile. The beech trees where Janet and Jim would meet the baddies, where Noddy came across the gollywogs in the middle of the night. She imagined being close to the beech trunks – polished bald men, baddies, bark shiny and stretched as a skin graft, whorls, the faces of gollies imprinted on the trunks. She turned her back on them and went through the inner hall to a small outer one, put her hand on the handle of the back door and got out. She'd go and camp with Ralph, this house was impossible to her. Audrey or no Audrey, she couldn't bear, wouldn't be able, to stick it out.

Peter was in the garden. 'No Joyce?' he asked awkwardly. 'Let me show you to your room.'

'You'll have to mind the stairs,' he warned her. 'See the sign.' Joyce's 'N' looked like an 'M'.

'Worm treads?'

'Not the clearest writing.' Peter was serious.

'Never mind,' she said. Ralph had told her that Joyce drank; Kate didn't blame her if she did.

'She's rather keen on notices,' Peter said. Kate had noticed the notices; the house was rigid with instructions and poorly written signs: TRESPASSERS WILL BE PROSECUTED/ABSOLUTELY NO ACCESS/NO TURNING/NO HAWKERS OR CIRCULARS. No this, no that. She remembered the notice for RF's funeral: NO FLOWERS. PLEASE SHUT THIS DOOR, TURN OFF THE IMMERSION. She looked at Peter. 'HANDLE IN GLOVED HAND?'

'The thing is not to hurry up and down, take it easy or you'll come a cropper. I shouldn't wear high heels.'

'I don't.'

'Oh. Well, good.'

He showed her the bedroom; to annoy him, she flopped extravagantly on the bed. 'You can't see out of the window from here,' she commented, but he was still going on, still worried about the stairs.

'You don't sleepwalk or anything?'

'I sleep like a log.'

'Good. You wouldn't want to sleepwalk out here.' He hovered half in, half out of the doorway.

'How is Audrey?' she asked, to stab him.

'A bit weak. Ralph went yesterday, he phoned today.'

'We ought to visit.'

'Well . . .'

'I might go with Ralph.'

74

'Yes, of course. Well, I'll let you get on, unpack. Don't forget the stairs.'

'I'm sure I'll be all right.' She looked about the cold room, hated it.

'Well, I'll leave you then.' Her baggage ranged along the circular wall.

'If you want to work while you're here, I'm sure we could find something that has a decent light.'

'Thank you.'

'We could sort it out in the morning if you like.'

'I might go to see Audrey in the morning.' Stab stab.

'Well, whenever. You're here now, that's the main thing.' He stood about, 'I'll leave you to it,' he repeated, and he did.

It's lovely here in the autumn, you must try and make it down for a weekend. Ralph would love to see you, and Joyce of course. Come down, bring a friend.

She didn't work, it didn't work. They didn't even argue – it wasn't the time or the place.

Audrey's illness, death and funeral, having Kate sitting quietly where he wanted her, in the garden on a chair, formed a circle into which Peter tried but failed to enter in. To be a member of the RF club you had to feel, to be both anxious and upset. Run when the phone rang, wring your hands when it didn't, you had to feel and, as Peter implied six months later in conversation with Nicola, he hadn't felt a thing.

Audrey died on 3 October 1983 and was buried in Glastonbury on a morning of brilliant sun. The remnants of the extended family dutifully showed up: Ralph and Kate, Hayward, Peter's publisher, Felix Switzer, Peter and old Joyce. Ralph and Kate were upset, Hayward and Felix were intrigued, Joyce played her part. It was only Peter who felt no relief that after three weeks of awkwardness the end of suffering had been reached.

A will drawn up in 1980, perhaps under the influence of RF, left the Newlyn House to Kate, the contents – 'Who needs it?' – to Peter. Ralph, faithful to the end but in

Audrey's eyes 'always the perfect fool', got nothing, par for the course for him. He and Kate had visited the hospital with religious regularity; for Peter, once had been enough. He had always felt out on a limb with Audrey, his mother's sister, his father's lover – *Must get Clem off my back*; seeing her incapable and dribbling in a chair could not alter this. A generalised distress at the indignities of old age was all he took away from that hospital visit, and the details of course, the details – lest we forget the elephantine legs placed as if they no longer belonged to her at an unnatural angle on the foot-rest of the ubiquitous wheelchair, Ralph making desperate desultory conversation, Kate holding Audrey's hopeless hand rather than his own. He remembered the hospital as being no better or worse than he'd expected, the atmosphere peculiar to such places of forever afternoon. Waiting in a TV lounge to be taken in to see his aunt: a cacophony of competing radios, a twenty-four inch television screen with Peter O'Sullevan's familiar voice riding above the rest, the rubber-soled squeak of passing nurses, hair off the forehead, nipped-in waists, a trolley in a corridor, the remains of soft-scoop mashed potato and greens. A scene orchestrated by the ghost of his father rather than any God, a scene in which he played a walk-on part.

Audrey didn't rage into death but, rather like the criminal Joyce considered her to be, went quietly and without fuss. Ralph, who was there, brought back her handbag, her sponge bag and her clothes, a letter from RF in her handbag that Peter chose not to read, a tissue parcel containing an alabaster egg marked 'Kate'.

Felix attended the funeral looking wealthy, well washed, his hands gleaming in the October sunlight, his voice oh-so-irritatingly bright. Hayward in a speckled, ill-pressed 'country suit' as inappropriate to the occasion as the tip he gave Peter as they filed out from the church: 'I've submitted *John Brown* for the CH Award'; always the businessman, he winked. Ralph, to whom Peter had had to lend a black tie, looking tearful but holding his stomach in . . . a sobbing Kate . . . Joyce in gloves and a felt hat, a brooch clasping the collars of her darkest knitted suit.

If no one else remembered anything in detail, if it was as they claimed to each other 'simply an awful blur', they need not have been concerned. Peter remembered everything. Peter walked with the whole lot buzzing in his head. Peter was a repository of family information, a custodian of Fox tradition, a mobile mausoleum of anything anyone could conceivably wish to know: feeling nothing, recording 'as it happened', remembering all.

The next, last? task was to drive Kate down to Newlyn to sort out about the house – he and Kate alone together for at least a hundred miles' drive in a car, alone give or take the odd ghost. Peter, who had been in and out of her room night after night these three weeks, Peter who had read her diary. Peter, who longed to absorb himself in the living and forget the recent dead, who had had three weeks of opportunity of potential pounce, had not dared so much as draw a claw. I want to take you away from all this, Kate, he thought in movietone as she got in beside him in the car and he prepared for the drive to Newlyn, taking her further and further in.

'It means it's going to be a good day, doesn't it?' Kate said, referring to the mist.

Peter put the key in the ignition. 'I've no idea.'

Peter had been up all night, sitting wound up in his armchair. Kate had slept like a log as usual; he hadn't had a wink. They drove cautiously into the mist through the empty lanes and got behind a milk tanker almost straight away.

'Oh Lord!'

Peter peered through the windscreen at the wipers; Kate looked out of the window into the white. It was cold in the car, they just ticked over behind the tanker, silence slipped between like the mist. Peter smoked without enjoyment as he had been doing virtually all night. They passed the tanker a mile on down a hill. Kate waved at the driver, Peter frowned at the wheel; the silence cemented between them – like Ralph, thought Peter, par for the bloody course.

Peter was opaque, Kate felt, like a drawing of a face without features. Where, at other times, with Felix, with her brother, with a friend, she would have prattled on, nervous that someone was not enjoying something, nervous chipping at the block, she let the block stand, blank granite, gazed through the window, thought of Audrey who had changed her life by leaving·her the house, thought of the house she'd been to before, three years ago with RF.

Peter didn't know what she was thinking but he had a fair idea, only disconnect, he longed to tell her, I'm here, look at me! Look at me! He looked at her, thought of taking his hand from the wheel to stroke that thick brown hair — 'one of the most beautiful and graceful and agreeable young women in London, only a little too fat'. Like Swift, loving didn't seem to be his strongest suit.

Audrey had sounded so young when RF talked about her; meeting her for the first time had been something of a shock. She'd seemed terribly old to Kate even then, terribly terribly old. RF had squeezed Kate's hand, perhaps in his own excitement, as this old woman with massive legs had appeared from the back of the house, now Kate's house, a mass of hens and sheds.

'Can I help?' she called from a distance, but coming closer she'd recognised RF and put her arms straight away around his waist and they had sat down together on a bench against the wall. The corn cup toppled, spilling, and hens poked about at her feet. She was crying and shooing the hens at the same time, one hand in RF's, the other dabbing at her eyes with the hem of an old plaid skirt. Huge elephantine legs in short fur boots. 'I'm so pleased,' she'd said again and again. Kate's armpits prickled with embarrassment. 'Thank you for coming. I'm so pleased.'

It had seemed so strange to Kate at twenty-five, Kate who couldn't imagine even middle-aged love, that this old woman should be so affected by the presence of this old man. Like seeing for the first time a piece of music you know well performed by a full orchestra, the pity of their love affair had come to Kate in waves and waves as she sat with the two of them trying to pretend she wasn't really there. It was a sobering experience for Kate and, although she knew enough of Richard already to realise that he would not have been able to face Audrey on his own, still she wished that having been a useful vehicle she could now make herself scarce. The house seemed tiny with Richard in it; it smelt of age and newspapers and cats, there was a pile of Mars Bars beside the television: 'I keep them for the children, they come in and out of here for sweets. I drink coffee these days, is that all right?'

Kate had made the coffee; the powdered milk was sogged with damp, the cups were rather dirty too.

'Now, Richard, if you go into that drawer you'll find all manner of things.'

Richard was reluctant but she insisted. 'There, you see, Clem.' She went through a pile of photographs. Kate brought the coffee and Audrey passed the photographs between them. 'The dead stay young. Look at this. There's Clem, that's Ig.'

'Is that Bournemouth?'

'Yes, it is! . . . Do you know Bournemouth?' she asked Kate, but did not wait for her reply. 'I believe it's dreadful now, full of geriatrics.' She laughed. 'There are places in America for us, Richard. We shouldn't like that, should we? I'm so glad you like the photographs. I made sure I kept them all. You didn't know I had them, did you? In divorce, you know, the fights over the photographs are the most splenetic.' She laughed again. 'Now you'll have to take this back for your memoirs, Richard. They are the past you see, the proof. I presume there will be memoirs?' she mocked him gently. Kate studied the carpet, which was filthy. 'Of course you'll write your memoirs, Richard, and I want you to have all these!

'I'm not lonely,' she said. It was obvious, from the way she talked ten to the dozen, that she was.

'I've a wonderful view here, Kate.' Kate looked towards the window. The sill was crowded, muddled with curtains, saucers, bits of cake. She'd seen so many paintings of clear views from windows but this was so interfered with so . . . 'I live in mess, my dreadful legs. I live downstairs, you see, I'm frightened of falling, that's always the way, isn't it, Richard?

Fall and break your hip and you're dead before the week's out. I prefer mess, mess in my own house. The woman next door's always on at me to move, you know. I want to stay alive, I shan't be going into any home. I'd die in a week, I know it. Anyway who would feed the hens? I'd love to see Peter . . . Don't misunderstand me, Richard, I'm not bitter, but I should have liked to see him growing up.' Tears clouded her eyes. 'Clem is in touch with me.' She shuffled the photographs like cards. 'You must take these photographs, Richard.'

He shook his head.

'When I'm dead, you must come back and take the lot, but take one now please . . .'

Kate had seen such photographs before. Photographs and old postcards, in junk shops, at auctions. It shook her.

'Perhaps you'd be my legs,' Audrey said, covering her embarrassment, handing Kate her empty cup.

'Just look at these old trunks. Now that you're here, I'd be a fool if I didn't ask you to do things for me. The old are like babies, Kate, that's the rub. You're still walking, Richard. I'd like it so much if you'd go to the top of the hill, like we used to do, and come down again and tell us all about it. Would you?' And when he left the room discreetly, she had cried.

'We used to be great walkers, the three of us, before Clem died. For years I couldn't forgive myself or him; you can't love to order, my dear. All an old muddle and a mess. In the end I suppose there's a sort of justice. He loved his work . . . I haven't seen him for some years. He doesn't write much now he's at The Round House. He's weak, you see, frightened stiff of Joyce. I missed his letters, there didn't seem to be . . .' Through the window they watched Richard on the hill. 'We had each other but only when he wasn't too preoccupied with work. Are you married?'

'No.'

'The only reason for marriage is children. Otherwise it's not worthwhile. Do drink your coffee, Kate. I'm like an old Arab when I get a chance to entertain.'

Kate felt miserable, felt that this woman could and would

80

see right through the clichés which kept rising in her mind as she watched Audrey so lonely and now so obviously upset. You've got such a lovely view here/children visit you/you can't be lonely with the hens/you've got such a good mind, it doesn't matter about your legs, the mess . . . Only recently she had read in the paper that there were now more people over seventy than ever before, a statistic; it hadn't mentioned how sad it all was – it hadn't occurred to her before, how sad, how terribly, terribly sad. She put the photographs away for Audrey, stuffed them into a drawer already stuffed – more papers, more clutter, more mess.

'Unfortunately I no longer have many correspondents . . . A great part of my life, living down here, has been writing letters. I'm a spinster; you may deduce from that what you will. I wouldn't have him unless I got the whole lot. He wasn't prepared for that; we wrote to each other instead. It was, in a way, sustaining . . . You haven't said, "You've got your memories." '

Kate smiled at her accuracy.

'Being old is like being in a wheelchair, one gets pushed around, they think you're soft in the head. Mad. Rather convenient for some of us, like Richard, the only opportunity we have of being mad, behaving selfishly, must grab it, madly selfish. One is forced to turn the whole thing on its head, turn disadvantage to advantage. I sincerely intend to be as mad as possible in the time remaining! Do you know Peter at all?'

'No, I don't.'

'Nor do I, nor do I. As children we were all brought up close by,' she said, skipping a generation. 'Our families were friends, we played together, you know how it is. I always loved Richard, even then. His sisters were dreadful; did you meet Nesta at all?'

'No.'

'Very much the bossyboots, even as a little girl.' Audrey laughed. 'Nesta and Joyce,' she placed two fingers together, 'like that. Richard chose Clem. It was bad for all of us, a mistake; she was only your age, perhaps a little older, when she died. He didn't really love me, you know, not in the same

81

way, not in the way that I loved him. We always lived apart. Men are queer creatures, don't you think? He was more loyal to Clem in death than he ever was when she was living. He had a conscience, developed a conscience, I suppose. Convenient. He tried to make me feel that what I wanted, needed from him, was absurd. He pretended to himself that I was crazy. I was in a way – crazy for him. He insulted my intelligence, still does. I always wanted to help him but he would protect himself, wouldn't let it happen, wouldn't let me in. Then of course there was his work, very convenient again and a sort of justice ... If I sound calm and reflective, I still don't really feel it, even at my age, even now.' She laughed and then grew sad again, serious once more. 'She wouldn't have died, I think, if I had married him instead. That's awfully hard to live with here, you see ... Now come on. I'll give you some eggs to take back with you.' Her thin hands stretched for Kate, who helped her to get up. 'The modern breeds won't sit, you know.'

'Like modern women.'

She laughed. 'Well, these are good old-fashioned broodies.'

'What do you do with the chicks?'

'Oh, that's the easiest part of all. I advertise them in the local rag: "Hens going cheap".' She giggled. 'There is always someone, especially in Cornwall. They're all self-sufficient, good-lifeish down here, old hippies, think hens have just been invented. It's easy to get rid of baby hens ...'

Richard still toiled on the hill, if it was too much for him, he didn't let it show. Audrey seemed at last to have talked herself out. Kate offered to sketch her; she agreed. 'I'm all right on the top half, aren't I?'

'More than all right,' said Kate.

'I came down here three years ago with your father,' Kate said now.

'You did more with him than I did.'

'I'm glad I can remember her as she was – as she was then, not in the hospital.'

'Absolutely.' His voice was cold.

'If you want me to feel guilty about the will, about the house, just say so.'

'I don't want you to feel guilty.'

'Good.'

'Do you think it's going to be upsetting?' she asked him but he did not reply. 'Will you take some stuff from the house?'

'I hadn't planned to. You may find it difficult to understand but I don't want any more stuff. I've got enough stuff, enough papers, enough photographs, enough old letters . . .'

'Enough for a book?'

'Who said anything about a book?'

'No one. Well, Joyce actually. Joyce, and Hayward mentioned it.'

'Not to me.'

'I suppose everyone just thinks you will. I mean, naturally enough . . .'

My good God, thought Peter, crossing the Tamar, heading west. Cornwall was everything he hated, now more than ever before. Even the motorway had a sort of seriously elemental promise that he really couldn't take. At Newlyn he made a great fuss about parking, strode off ahead of Kate, ignored the woman who hailed him from the next-door garden, marched straight up the path and into the cottage, slamming the door behind him.

He wouldn't let me in, Kate thought, remembering Audrey's phrase, but she said nothing. Let it happen, let him go alone. She lingered instead in the garden, talked to the woman on the other end of the terrace who stood leaning heavily on a zimmer walker looking her suspiciously up and down.

'Ten minutes' walk to the town,' the woman claimed in a London accent. 'Not everyone's cup of tea by a long chalk. Your husband's not interested in gardening then?'

Inside the house Peter looked deathly, like a bit of chalk himself.

'We'll have to organise house clearers,' he said icily, unapproachable. 'I've no intention of going through all this.'

83

This side of your father's life is so distasteful to you, isn't it? Coming here for you is like a sort of owning up, she wanted to say, but you're not big enough for it, are you; you're weak. Instead she said, 'Okay. Fine. And we must get something for the woman next door, for taking care of things.'

Peter stood helpless at the cluttered window: a wooden spoon, a hairbrush, a rusted tin of Players Medium Navy Cut.

'We could have a bonfire,' Kate suggested, 'Get rid of the clothes at least.' She unbolted the back door and went outside. 'The woman next door says the cat's gone missing.'

'Great. Great. And what the hell do we do about the hens?' Peter shouted after her.

'Take them back.'

'You're joking.'

'Calm down, Peter, for goodness sake calm down. I'll cope. We'll put them in a box, put them in the boot of the car. There's plenty of space at The Round House . . .'

He was hopeless, helpless. She went in and took over, took his arm. 'We'll do an hour or so, start a bonfire, go to a pub for lunch, organise house clearers . . .'

They sat outside a pub drinking whisky; a couple at another table silently worked their way through a measly ploughman's lunch. The woman took the man's pickled onion, he wiped her face with his napkin.

'That's couples for you,' Peter commented.

'It looks all right to me.'. . .

'We'll have to wait for the hens to go to roost,' Kate said later. 'We'll never catch them now.'

'What do we do now?'

'We could go for a walk by the sea.'

'Not the sea.'

'Along the cliff then?'

She took his hand as they walked; he was distant to her but she knew, just as she had known when RF had taken her hand those years ago at Audrey's, that he was, for this moment at least, dependent upon her.

She told him about her earlier visit, the photographs of his mother, Bournemouth. 'He never took me to Bournemouth,' Peter said.

'You could go now.'

'Yes, of course I could.' Even he smiled at the idea. 'The time we spent together, everything we did, was, I suppose you'd call it, educational. The way he trucked me up and down hill forts, like training for the SAS. I longed to go to Bournemouth or Weymouth or Weston-super-mare. I wanted to have fun, ice cream, somewhere with people in it.' He shook his fist into the October air. 'You went to Bournemouth; why the hell wouldn't you take me?'

Kate grinned. 'Well, I went. David and I went to all those places, family holidays with a vengeance – I think you probably got off lightly. If your memories are punctuated by stiff walks, mine are of having my hand held, tightly. A walk along a path through an interesting wood that we were never allowed to explore: it bites, it stings, be careful! Smocked dresses that were tight under the arms even then, white socks. I'd want to go off and lie in a patch of bluebells and daddy would pick me one, one to smell.

'Is that memory *Daring Miss Pears*?'

'Yes, partly it is.'

Kate was silent because she wanted him to talk; getting Peter to talk was like getting someone down from a high building. She felt that in some ridiculous Lawrentian way he was resisting her, and as they walked now along the fringes of a golf course the balance swung between them as she tried to talk him down. The sea on that blowy, cloudy afternoon reflected her feelings: familiar and reassuring when the sun shone on it, grey and nasty when the clouds obscured the sun; even the gulls sounded different without the sun – without the sun they were simply scavengers, their longing calls a tearing, empty wail. Peter talked. He apologised for his behaviour in the house, he agreed to take the hens back in the car. She did not let go of his hand.

Later they lay on the spongy grass watching the empty

beach below. Again she felt for his hand, but now he wouldn't give it, lit a cigarette.

'I'm quite all right,' he said pompously. 'I do wish you'd stop treating me as if I were upset.'

'It wouldn't surprise me if you were upset,' she said reasonably, 'considering all the things that have happened to you this year. There's nothing shameful about showing that you're upset.'

'God.' He crushed the cigarette into the grass, got up.

In the car he opened up again, told her about his mother's death, how it had been after the war, just a parent of a different sex, how it had seemed to him then. On the fringes of Newlyn they stopped at a nursery. Kate brought a rather funereal white cyclamen for the woman in the zimmer frame and a small tree, which she gave to him.

'What is it, bonzai?'

'Read the label.'

'You read it.'

She read it out to him: 'Giant Redwood Wellingtonia. Plant a tree and improve your environment.'

'You think my environment needs improving?'

'I definitely do.'

They drove the journey back to The Round House, silence growing between them once again; she held his hand for a moment before getting out of the car.

'I'll deal with the hens,' she said.

'I don't know what you're going to do with them.'

'I'll put them in the pigsty.'

'Won't they need straw or something? Perches?'

'Not tonight.'

'I'll help you.'

'I'll do it.'

'I'll make some coffee for you.'

'Thank you.'

The house was quiet. He went to the sitting room but Joyce was already in bed. He stood with his hand on the kettle in the kitchen, as hopeless as he'd been at Audrey's window. Kate, coming in, tiptoed up and kissed him on the cheek.

'Don't do that.'

'Did it give you a shock?'

She kissed him again. She put her arms round his neck and held him.

'Coffee,' he said, breaking away.

'No.' Her voice was leaden with reproach.

'Going to bed?'

'Yes.'

'Well, it has been a long day,' he said stupidly. 'The kettle's boiled if you want coffee,' he added, although she had already left the room, left him, disgusted by him, gone.

Much shaken, Peter drank the coffee on his own. 'Hell hath no fury . . .' He poured the dregs down the plughole, washed his cup. Unable to help himself, he went on to scour the sink, wipe the fridge, attend to the neck of the Squeezy bottle, which was gummy — delaying tactics, sweet, old friends. Up to his own room rather than Kate's. Kate heard him coming, his tread on the stone stairs. How she loathed every hair on his head! Nothing changes, nothing changes. He pulled the covers from his bed and settled down to spend the evening huddled in his armchair. He would buy her a present, anything she wanted, something big, Christmas time for Kate. He would give her something in the morning, for he couldn't give himself.

At four in the morning he crossed the floor to her room and looked at her for a long time. She slept like a baby not a log, unguarded, her arms beside her head on the pillow. The fingers, the hand he had held with the little dent between the finger and the thumb: how he longed to put his finger there, stroke the shallow space. He cleared his throat and she turned towards him, her eyes open. He put his fingers to his lips.

'What?' she asked, half asleep.

'Nothing.'

They looked at each other in the dark.

'Are you coming in?'

He nodded but still stood there like an ape.

'Well, come on then, don't be pathetic, Peter.'

He got into the bed beside her. 'Cold,' he said before she silenced him, took him in her large, frighteningly capable, braceleted arms.

Kate woke alone. She remembered the night before, the middle of the night. Allelulia! she thought, stretching in the bed. At last! At last! And the day in Cornwall: Peter the fortress allowing himself to be besieged. Half asleep, half awake she lay. Yesterday came to her, to her palm – yesterday and loving Peter – an oval, smooth shape as perfect as an egg. The oval of a newly laid, promising, perfect egg, an egg, an egg. She remembered the fragments of her dream:

She had woken with something delicate in her hand. Opening it, so gently, she had discovered the perfectly shaped egg. Off she'd gone to Peter's room, across the corridor with the egg. He lay in bed, like an effigy, a stone. In she went, in to him. Holding the love with one hand in her palm, she kissed him.

'Don't do that.'

'Did it give you a shock?'

'Peter's dead,' Joyce said. 'And I've got rid of that ridiculous tree. We can't have a tree that size in a garden like this. It would shade my borders terribly. You might at least have come to me for a little advice.' Joyce's Scots voice. They stood in the dead man's room. 'You've got something in your hand, Kate. What is it? Give it here. Let me see.' Kate put her hand behind her back. Joyce would drop it, Joyce dropped everything. Joyce was Mrs Danvers and she wagged a crippled finger at poor Kate. 'Come on.' The voice was brisk. 'Give me that.' It was fragile, precious, perfect, beautiful, but Joyce brought her arm forward, forcing open the fingers, relieved her of the egg. 'Really!' Still holding tight to Kate's arm, she had taken her across to the window, made her watch while she hurled the egg out and down, down. And Kate had run and run and run in her dream, down the worn treads of the stairs, outside in the October morning to see her own egg smashed and shattered, fragments, splinters of white alabaster, unproductive, sterile, not a hint of yoke or white,

as dead as Peter in bed, dead, delph egg. 'He's been dead for at least a year, dear. I'm surprised you didn't notice, you didn't know. Oh, he's been dead for ages now, technically, terribly dead.'

Kate sat up shaking, trying to forget, determined to forget, she went downstairs. But in that clammy, high-ceilinged kitchen it came to her again; the egg was in her hand again and she couldn't keep it to herself. Hastily she made a cup of tea and took it upstairs – she remembered yesterday didn't she? Last night? She and Peter, allelulia, lovers and at last! It was all right between them, all right for her to walk straight into his room.

He was lying in bed, and from the moment that she saw him she knew, as she had known during her walk round The Round House on her own that first afternoon, that though parts of it were right the rest of it was wrong, wrong. Wrong when she had to move his books to the floor to make room on the bedside table, wrong to put the cup down, wrong in this circular room to squeeze past the bed to get to the window to see if her dream would come true – the window that looked into the heights of the beech trees waving their arms, naked without leaves.

Wrong. But if you're running, her mind ran as she placed the cup, there's no emergency stop and you plough on through a pedestrian crossing full of schoolchildren, you can't stop. Wrong. His things – and she remembered too late the letters on the hall table – what have I got to do with these things? And he hadn't spoken, the pompous sod; it would be better if indeed he had been dead. Laugh at me and look out on your beeches. Oh God, she realised now that she could no longer feel the egg! Where was the egg, where was it? Frantic now, she looked into her hand but the palm was empty and, worse, she could now hardly remember cupping her hand for it, feeling its firmness, the sense of it, knowing it was really there – like the dream it was rolling away, here in his room. Why didn't he say anything? How long had she stood there empty-handed? How long had he watched her stand? Dear God, she was stunned by the error of her ways.

She left the window, passed the bed, the teacup, and at last she made it to the door. She sang under her breath as she went downstairs, the sort of song you sing when the house is burning down around you. She phoned Felix and told him to come 'now, straight away'. She collected her things from the bedroom she hated and waited outside like a maid dismissed, as far from the house as possible, near the gate by the road. NO TURNING/NO TRESPASSERS. She waited for over two hours, just stood. But at last here came Felix, urbane, grown-up, helping her load her things into the boot of the car, driving away.

'Could you stop,' she asked him barely a mile from the house, and he did so, pulling in at a lay-by in the next village where a straggle of passengers descended from the Saturday bus. 'Hang on a moment.' Kate got out of the car and proceeded to fiddle for a minute or two at her bundle of possessions in the boot, returning to the front seat, putting on her seatbelt, Audrey's delph egg cupped in the palm of her hand. 'Okay,' she said.

'What do you want to do?' he asked her, though he had never seen her so distressed, though he felt at this moment she was incapable of deciding. 'Come on, sweetie. It can't be as bad as that.' He stroked her free hand, tried to calm her. He hoped she wasn't going to cry and also couldn't help himself hoping that she wasn't going to smoke – poor Felix just couldn't tolerate smoking in a car. 'Never make decisions when you're in a state,' he advised her, noticing the loose bits of skin on the hand he now held, the bits she'd bitten or picked at around an already closely bitten nail. 'You can't win them all,' he said into the silence and then, taking the initiative, started the engine up, drove on.

You can't win them all, he thought, and settled briefly into a silence and a sadness of his own. Kate was very young, it was easy to overlook that; age and experience had taught Felix that you couldn't win them all, but was it common sense or cowardice, cynicism that settled for a philosophy like that?

8

'You should have married her,' said Nicola, on her fourth vodka in the nearest, least offensive local pub. 'Hughie says living together is too fainthearted, and I think he's absolutely right. You've got to commit yourself, I think, don't you? Relationships and all the rest of it, it's so second-rate.' Peter looked all right but she suspected him of being morose, she jollied him along. It had been a red-letter day for Peter and she would not let it go unsung.

In the morning he had received two letters, the first saying he'd been awarded the Curry-Hoare Prize for the best biography of 1983, for the book lampooned in the *Spectator*, 'Salad King'. In the second letter was an invitation from the Open University proposing he write a set of preliminary study books on the art of research. A third letter, which reached him indirectly later on, was in his pocket now and he drank with Nicola to get rid of its added weight.

'Something for you in the afternoon post,' he'd said to her. 'Your turn.'

'Thanks. Afternoon post. I do like staying here; in London afternoon post is a thing of the past.'

'Mustn't become too preoccupied with the past,' he'd said. He smiled, she smiled.

Nicola opened her envelope. Inside was a cellophane-wrapped card and a covering note from her husband. She looked at it briefly, talking all the time.

'Actually, part of it's for you,' she said and handed the card to him. 'Look.'

He looked.

'It's been nagging me ever since the first day I came down

to lunch. I knew I'd seen it somewhere but I just couldn't for the life of me remember, then it just clicked. I asked Hughie to see if he could get it for me . . .'

Peter looked hard at the card, a trump. 'Where exactly?'

'In Smith's. I saw it in Oxford but H. must have got it in London. A day or so before I came down here I'd been out to dinner, a history society thing, in Oxford. Barry Cunliffe had been speaking, his formal-gardening thing. I expect you know Barry? Anyway, I dashed into Smith's the next day. I was on a double yellow line and there was a whole series of cards. I bought something else, one of the series . . .'

'Series?'

'Oh yes, there were half a dozen or so.'

'I see.'

'And then I drove down here that Friday and the minute I saw the fruit cage I realised it was the same one. The trouble was I couldn't then remember where I'd seen it before. Then I was so excited about doing your father and everything it simply went out of my mind . . . It's really sweet of Hughie to go to so much trouble for me; he usually makes a mock of my famous coincidences, but even he admitted that this one really is quite odd . . .'

Peter nodded at Nicola as she talked; all she needed in full-spate like this was the occasional benevolent nod. Nasty pieces of hurt, they felt granular and indigestible, seemed stuck in his throat. He attempted to pass the card back to Nicola but she protested.

'Have it, honestly. It's for you.'

Peter turned the picture away from him and read the back: No Greeting. *The Fruit Cage*, Kate Whittaker, Camden Graphics 1984. Must be hard up, he thought.

'It is the same one, isn't it?'

'Yes.'

'You haven't already got it or anything, have you? I wanted it to be a surprise.'

'A day full of surprises,' said Peter.

'Yes, isn't it great? You ought to get the whole set. I can't remember exactly what the others are. Hens, I sent Barry the hens; he keeps Gloucester Spots, pigs not hens, but he's a member of that thingie, you know, about keeping old breeds going . . .'

'Rare breeds.'

'That's the one.' She went on and on. Peter put the card in his pocket, felt it weigh him down.

'Who is this Kate then?'

'An old friend of the family, one of my father's famous protégées.'

'Oh, I see, oh . . . Do you think she should go in, Peter?' Nicola's tone had changed. 'I didn't put her in the herring pile, did I?'

'You probably did, but I don't think it's important.'

'Sure?'

'Absolutely.'

'Perhaps I ought to look at that pile, take it up to London with me, or look at it down here. Will you remind me, Peter? Don't forget, Kate Whittaker. Right. I've got so much to think about at the moment I'm very likely to forget. I'll make a note of it. Remind me to look at the note.'

'So you didn't want to marry Kate,' Nicola probed, as they celebrated in the pub.

'I didn't think about it.'

'Of course you didn't, men rarely do. I bet she did.'

'Well, we'll never know.'

He attempted to end the conversation but she said, 'If you go on like that, no one will have you anyway; you are a fool sometimes. You must have had offers, surely?'

'I had one.'

'Tell me, please, go on, I love gossip.'

Because he liked her he told, and embellished in the telling, the story of the Belgian poetess. It wasn't Nicola's fault that the card had proved a clumsy gesture, and fool or not he felt he had fooled her into thinking that Miss Whittaker's rendering of his fruit cage hadn't really hurt.

He told her that he'd had a very busy year, 1975; he was writing about the Garston sisters (she nodded, she had read the book) when he'd fallen, at the time it seemed hoplessly, in love with Paulette.

'Paulette! I don't believe you.'

'Well, the name doesn't really matter.'

'I hope you're not making all this up.'

'I am,' he lied. 'I'm doing it to amuse you. Anyway she worked part time in a pet shop on the Fulham Road.' He'd hovered for weeks, talked about gerbils, almost committed himself to a family of Dutch dwarfs – 'rabbits,' he explained – when out of the blue she suggested they get married.

'What happened then?'

'I panicked. I said I couldn't have the rabbits because I'd suddenly been landed with a vicious Chinese dog. I called it the "telephone dog". Actually, it used to bring in hedgehogs when she was on the phone – "Have to go, hedgehog trouble." Then the dog was so vicious that I had to talk to her through the window if she came round.'

'I don't believe it.'

'She did. After all the pet-shop hovering, she had got me down as a mad pet lover. It got me out of the rabbits. "Let the dog see the rabbit," that sort of thing.'

'Did that finish it?'

Peter smiled at Nicola. 'Not quite. I thought of telling her I was already married and baulked at the prospect of bigamy, but then one evening it ended for me by itself. We were in a pub at the time. She couldn't come home with me because of the dog, and I decided that I couldn't love a woman who loved crisps.'

Nicola was eating crisps. She giggled. 'I'm safe then?'

'You are a married woman.'

'Honestly, Peter, I do believe you made the whole thing up.'

'Well, I didn't want you to think that no one found me desirable.'

'Whoever said anything about that. I think you're extremely desirable.'

'You don't!'

'Honestly, I do.'

Desirable or not, it was Nicola's turn to have a quiet word with Joyce. She helped wash up the cups and saucers of morning coffee, and being Nicola she didn't drop a thing.

'I rather think he's brooding,' she said in her loud and definite voice. Anyone with their head in the fireplace would have got an earful of what she said, but Nicola did not believe in lowered voices or secrets; deceit, like relationships, that sort of thing, awfully second-rate.

They discussed the card and its implications.

'I wonder if it might be better if he went away?'

They discussed the idea of Peter going away.

As they talked, one got the impression of a piece of furniture being moved from one room to another, of something being shifted, being stored. Joyce was very helpful; administration had always been her line.

Peter was a major irritation to Joyce and it was not surprising that she thought his removal, albeit temporary, quite the thing. In her eyes the handover had gone well; she had calculated it with all the seriousness of an exchange of spies, superficially everything had gone as planned. But Joyce, the lady of the lasting knitted suits, Joyce the needlewoman of old, knew that, though the right side of her latest handiwork passed muster, the back was still a mess. Seeing Peter in the garden, loping about, going off and coming back from his, to her eyes, absolutely purposeless walks, irritated her, and irritation wasn't healthy, wasn't good. Although she did not say this to Nicola but to Ralph, talent was no good without ambition, determination and drive. Peter, prize or no prize, lacked the qualities she had so admired in his father. He did not contribute, he was worrying, he did not seem to be moving forward, he was irritating. Having sorted out the biography, Joyce's appetite to clear the decks was stronger than ever. Peter and Ralph — untidy stitches, loose ends.

'Well, he could go away now, I suppose; he's got the money for it, and there's nothing really for him here. Would it suit you better, Nicola?'

'In a way,' thinking of his desirability, 'in a way I think it would. Really it's him I worry about,' she said truthfully. 'I feel the past is rather a dead hand on him.'

'He hasn't worked properly, you know, since it happened,' Joyce said.

'I rather gathered that. Perhaps he feels there are too many memories down here, feels he can't work here . . .'

Joyce's body was stooped and cobbled with arthritis but her mind fairly whizzed as they talked. Her mind leapt always to money, and it occurred to her that solving the problem of Peter also affected the cottage and Ralph. With Peter away, Ralph could move in with her. 'I may tell you, Nicola, that RF had plans for that cottage that I, for one, would dearly love to see fulfilled. He always wanted it as a study centre for students. The cottage needs seeing to but I think we could get a grant, one of RF's dreams . . .'

'Surely it would be awkward for you though, Joyce, you living here alone with Ralph.'

'The devil you know, Nicola. I've spent my life living with men. I think I can cope with Ralph. Perhaps I should have a word with Hayward. . .'

'Hayward?'

'Peter's publisher. More than that of course, his father was an old, old friend.'

'I don't think we ought to be too pushy, Joyce.'

'Of course not, dear, but if two women can't organise one man I don't know anyone who can.'

If Peter looked so irritating to Joyce it was because he was waiting for something, anything, to turn up. The fact that no one is indispensable is well known, yet nevertheless unpalatable when it applies to you. Peter was not immediately consulted about his 'holiday' but in a day or so he began to get the drift. Still he dithered, drifted in an increasingly heavy sea. The sense that his father might be hiding, might have a last word for his ears only, made him stay. He might be hiding, just out of sight, just out of earshot; there could be another herring somewhere up that undoubtedly capacious sleeve.

Several times Peter crept into the sun room when it was

unoccupied and challenged his father to come out, but there was nothing doing, no whisper of a message for his ears only coming from beyond the grave. He told himself that the part of his life that had bound him so awkwardly to his father was now finished. Nicola would see to everything; he could go away. No longer needed as custodian, now simply someone who was rather in the way, he caught the drift of their conversation, he felt miserable and alone.

Yes, he now had freedom, the freedom of the loose end. If he wanted to drift he could drift, but not here, they suggested; please Peter, somewhere else, not under our feet, not here. Nicola's timely intervention had brought him down at last from the hill fort; he had descended to the ramparts, where he now went round and round. Blessed are the meek for they give away their fathers without fuss and so diminish themselves. Having carried the weight for so long, he now felt positively lopsided, despite appearances – so courteous to Nicola, so polite to Joyce and Ralph. He felt as Audrey had felt in the Newlyn house: frightened of falling down. He sat about, he walked around, he hardly needed any sleep. He recalled passages from Kate's diary:

Life the same here if not more so, residents move, more apart than together, like a wretched stately dance, weaving in and out of one another, hands don't touch. Find myself getting caught in the stasis, nodding at Peter, listening to Joyce, waving a hand at Ralph's retreating back. Now when I talk they're not the words I wanted to say, comes out stilted, can't be spontaneous, catches in my throat – is catches the word? – is it catching, frightened of becoming like them . . .

In his bedroom, for lack of anything better to do, he sorted through Audrey's letters to his father and his to her, returned. He put them into sequence, taking a bitter pleasure from the task; the invisible worm, love growing sour and weakly, reading disenchantment between the lines.

Coffee times were now taken up with discussion of what Peter should do – or, more precisely, where exactly he should go. Ralph played a supportive role in the discussion; as a homosexual, the grass for him had always been the same shade of green. For him, going away lost its excitement if it meant also coming back. Escape was an illusion, an improbability, but in front of the women this he dared not say. For the ladies were less lyrical, more practical, past masters in arranging things for other people, other men. In their hands the discussion moved in minutes from 'if' and on to 'where' and 'when'. Nicola, who was frequently inspired by glossy and expensive magazines, went for Italy in a big way. She, with the backing of *Harpers and Queen*, recommended the efficacy of Tuscan farmhouses as one would a back rub or a pill. As a member of the English upper-middle class, Nicola suggested things that would have brought tears to the eyes of Kate's guiltily middle-class member of the Blackbird board. Nicola had connections everywhere, and a Fox of course only had to say the word to have it made flesh. Contacts abounded; interesting people with good books and full booze cupboards peopled Tuscany these days. Castellina in Chianti, the Berrys were right there – ten miles of vines and olives, looking towards Siena, so much sun ... Peter and Pepita Perry-Smith had a magnificent conversion job somewhere on the hills above Lucca ... Now Vecoli, what about Vecoli? Nicola was inspired by the Anglo-Tuscan love affair – wonderful skies, she said, mentioning Shelley. Peter thought about Tennyson and the Isle of Wight.

Goodwill surrounded Peter now that he had given up the ghost. A walking holiday in the Alps might suit him. Brochures were solicited from the local branch of Carefree, opinions of friends were sought, compatible companions around the globe suggested. Coffee time sparkled with talk of Malta, Ibiza and other islands; had he thought seriously of Sark? Ralph's sticky biro now circled travel columns in the *Telegraph* – 'This might be of interest.' All go.

He had the money, no ties; he had his commission, he was free. They rejoiced in his new freedom, well deserved they said, well after the event. The prize was the breakthrough he'd been waiting for; he'd been obviously waiting for something – it must have been the prize. Money to spend, money to invest, why the Open University hadn't thought of him before now ... There were spin-offs for everyone, everyone rejoiced. Allelulia! At last! At last! At last! Ralph's cottage could be turned into a study centre: fieldwork, a minibus, grants, grants, grants, money, money, money, and Peter out of the house. Peter out of the sun room, and Nicola could get her grubbies on the herring pile for that thorough poke-about; Peter out of the sun room, Peter out of the way. Even the Uneedus boy put his oar in, for everybody knew – famous son fêted, Salad King dressed: 'I'd go away old son,' he told Peter. 'Definitely,' he said, with that odd spacing he gave to words of more than one syllable. 'Def-in-itely.'

It was a niggling disappointment to all concerned that Peter seemed unable to decide quite where to go, but 'choice is one of the hardest things to cope with' Nicola told Joyce and Joyce, who hadn't had much choice up to now, categorically agreed. Only Ralph, who had been denied choice throughout his life, was subdued in his importuning of this now doubly-famous son. He did indeed mark the travel in the *Telegraph* but he was not entirely happy about what he did. In the company of such practical and definite women, it seemed bad manners, if nothing else, to waver, but there was a wobble in those biro lines, a secret little dread.

'And the more you do the more you're capable of,' Nicola reflected, returning to The Round House after dashing off with a late letter to Hugh. This was a note about the sofa – about the consumer programme that had mentioned the Upholsterers' Guild – instructions and an address to Hughie about where to write re their troubled chesterfield, with the threat, again mentioned in the programme, about taking the whole thing to the Small Claims Court. Oddly, although it was quite a business being stuck in the countryside, neither Hughie nor the sofa struck Nicola as being in any way remote. She was good on perspective; she was down here doing a job; life went on.

'I do think it's a good thing when choices are almost made for you,' she said to Peter, thinking how cold his room was, concentrating her considerable warmth on him. Peter was going at last, tomorrow he would be off. Nicola sat on his bedroom windowsill while he packed. Packed? Well she saw at once that he was wavering a bit, that she would have to urge him on. The case on the bed was empty apart from a cellophane pack of Bic razors provided earlier by Joyce. 'Come on,' she encouraged him, looking pointedly at the empty case. 'You can do better than that.'

Embarrassed by her presence in a room full of hidden, secret things, Peter made an effort, fiddled with the folds in a pair of socks, put them in with the razors, feeling Kate's card in his pocket, a socking blow. He placed the socks in the elastic pocket of the suitcase, flicked the elastic as she spoke.

'You've been up here for ages, Peter. What have you been doing all the time?'

Well, he'd been stuffing *The Journey from A* and the dressing-gown sleeve and the letters from Audrey and Kate and the tracing of the mirror into the briefcases, but this he could hardly say.

'I've been doing a bit of catching-up on Audrey, discreetly of course,' Nicola informed him now with deadly precision. 'What else can you tell me about her?'

'Nothing. Not very much. We were rather kept apart.' By the time the cock crows . . . 'She's more a friend of Ralph's.'

'And Kate's, obviously.'

'Yes, Kate.'

'Extraordinary to leave her that house, don't you think? I bet your father put her up to it. Audrey, I mean, not Kate.'

'Possibly.'

'And Kate's living down there now.'

'Is she? I didn't know that.'

'According to Ralph.'

'Really.' Peter sounded noncommittal, the shake of his hands embarrassingly evident even in the collection of the socks.

'I'd like to know more about Audrey, it's so tricky when everyone's dead. When one can't get information from the horse's mouth . . . It's not always easy to get at the truth.'

100

'I shouldn't worry about it.'

'Of course I worry about it. Honestly, I worry about you sometimes, Peter. Cynicism is too easy, it's a trap; you don't want to fall into that.'

Peter wanted to fall into his suitcase, fold himself up and shut the lid, but the conversation, as conversations did with Nicola leading them, continued on and on.

'Ralph's been trying to corner you.'

'I know that.'

'You ought to make the effort to have a word with him before you go. He told me he wanted a word –'

'Probably more than one.'

Nicola sighed; he *was* naughty. She folded her legs comfortably on the sill. 'It would be a nice gesture if you asked him to take you to the train.'

'I'm not going by train.'

'What! Oh, Peter, you can't go by car. You can't possibly. Think of the hassle. You'd have to park it, leave it somewhere, it would cost the earth. You can't go by car.'

'But I want to go by car.' Peter felt like a child, miserable and easily defeated. Not knowing where he was going, he thought of the car as a kind of travelling cupboard, a vehicle to put his life into during his stay away.

'You won't need it,' Nicola insisted.

'What about all my stuff?'

'What stuff? Three pairs of socks and a packet of razors?'

'You know what I mean.' He felt cross now.

'Well, you won't need much.'

Cross and increasingly pathetic.

'Let me do it,' she suggested. 'Shirts?' Nicola took over the packing. In a way he felt relieved. He sat down on the windowsill, she went to the case. 'Have you decided exactly where you're going?'

'I haven't had much time to think about it.'

She wondered what he had been thinking about. 'In some ways there's nothing to beat Britain,' she said. 'Cheaper, too.'

'I thought you favoured Tuscany.'

'Well. One is always a bit unrealistic when one first gets money, don't you think?'

'I've no idea.'

'If I had the time, I think I'd do a tour of the British Isles. There are so many places one always means to visit . . .'

'What are you suggesting, Nicola? The Norfolk broads?'

'Why not? Or the Western Isles or something. Your father was interested in Angelsea –'

'He was also interested in Calshot Spit.'

'Yes, well. But Cornwall's nice . . .' Nicola had given up Alice bands and taken to hair combs; she replaced one expertly in her luxuriant hair. 'And –'

'And what?'

'And you could visit Kate.'

'I don't want to visit Kate.'

'Just to see how she's settling in. Cornwall's lovely –'

'No, it isn't.'

'Do you want these folded?' Nicola said crossly.

'If you like.' He was niggled too. The sense of being married to Nicola that he'd often had in the sun room – 'Have you seen the hoover?'. 'Do you want these folded?' – coaxed Peter and made it difficult for him to resist. Nicola now expounded about Cornwall, about Kate. 'I'm probably the last person she wants to see,' he protested.

'Rubbish. I'm sure she'd love to see you.'

'Nicola, you've never even met her. How can you say that?' But, God, he felt pathetic, wrapped his legs closer round him on the windowsill. 'Why?' he asked. 'Why do you think she would?'

'Well, you know.'

'I don't.'

'Ralph said –'

But the mention of Ralph, the thought of that decrepit receiving letters from Kate – visits, was it? – under a blanket, whatever. No. He wouldn't get involved again. 'If you've taken over the packing, I'll go and see Ralph,' he said.

'Don't get all uppity.'

'I am not uppity.'

102

'He's in a terrible state about his roof, you know,' Nicola informed him as he went, uppity, to go downstairs.

'I didn't know.'

'Oh yes. Apparently water's getting in.'

'What, now?'

'So he says. He's got buckets and everything he . . .'

Peter shut the door, firmly, quietly. Downstairs, taking a stick from the crocodile, he went outside in the rain to walk – 'still alive, took a little walk, *d'un humeur d'un chien*. Saw everything *en noir*.' Actually he saw everything rather clearly. He did what he never did: walked high to a vantage point, turned and looked down at The Round House, solid in its distant dip. He was leaving it tomorrow, saying good-bye.

A large, round, unremitting building – what had he said to Nicola that first day in the fireplace? 'Fortitude', forever, forbear. The chilly, polished horror of flagged floors, attics, cellars, and particularly passageways in which to pass Joyce and not talk to her, gardens in which to avoid Ralph. The tower bedrooms: *How can something so rounded be simultaneously so stern?* Kate had written in her diary. The double doors into the main hall, the croc, the conservatory. Peter knew every room, where Joyce's dried flowers hung: *Preserving everything, including me*, his father had written in despair. Joyce dropping the milk pan, clang; Ralph spooning more sugar into his cup; Nicola working in the sun room; no one was indispensable, perspective's lesson, life went on. Perhaps that was what his father had thought, had known, had learnt in his years down there in the dip: with or without him, life went on. When Ralph died, when Joyce died, Peter would, under the details of his father's will, be entitled to sell the cottage and the house, but would the sounds go on in it when it was over, over and emptied out – the clang of the milk pan, the words rebounding from the blank round walls, fortitude, forbearance? The house, the house, the bloody house. So old, so crammed, so full – built on a site (he imagined the voice of Huw Wheldon) where other buildings had stood, unremitting history beneath it, around it, accreted to it. *People are trapped in history and history is trapped in them.* Sickeningly, suffocatingly, stuffed.

As he'd stood in the narrow circular passageways it had been easy to imagine his father shadowing him, his dead mother cradling him, postcards from Audrey waiting on the silver salver in the hall; the bustling whiskery figure of Nesta with a skirt full of keys walking in the house where she'd once held sway. The fruit cage where he'd got stuck as a child would soon begin to bud again and bulge, the netting would be replaced, a wind would catch the wisteria. Kate had painted the cage and strangers would go into W.H. Smith's, buy the card, send the card along. Nesta pulling him out of the fruit cage, Peter in the scullery being sick. 'Like the anguish before nausea only spiritual,' Tolstoy had written about his state. 'I go to bed with anguish in my heart, and I wake up with the same anguish. I just cannot overcome it.' RF had read that. Had he felt it too: a smaller man living in a dip considers going for a dip? People in circular passageways; Nesta thwarting Joyce, Joyce thwarting Audrey, Audrey thwarting Clem. Nesta unable and, according to all accounts, pathologically unwilling, to delegate the house to her brother or to any other woman. Nesta and Joyce between them squeezing his mother into an early grave; RF with Audrey, having it off, in Crete. Nesta had tugged and pulled him from the cage, holding tight to all she could in her life, had – and how she would hate to know it – left no gap. That was the worst of it, no gap.

The house observed from this height through the falling rain: the sense of gaps being filled again, of history repeating itself or simply going on. Unrivalled now, Joyce continued the tradition – the coffee for Ralph, the note for the fish. Peter stood getting soaked, looking down; the sea went out but it returned and filled the rock pools once again. Who to know whether this water that brought back life was the same or different, so similar was it to what had come and gone before, doing the same work. It didn't really matter, poor Nesta, it didn't matter at all. Only the stone changed, 'my heart contracted', the water eventually eroded the little rock.

It was still raining slightly when Peter went to see what it was Nicola thought he 'ought' to do for Ralph. Although only six in the evening, the garden was shot by that odd dead light so difficult to drive in, a mass of dark blowing clouds, a weak May sun glinting through the beaches at the back. *The rain goes on longer here than anywhere else*, Kate had written, *drips on and on through the leaves of the rhododendrons*. Peter trod gingerly over a fallen branch on the path to the cottage. Avoiding Ralph had meant avoiding the cottage; Peter noticed guiltily the three/four missing slates on the roof. He'd arranged for the Uneedus boy to tackle things. He did what he ought to have done before, but did not now want to linger in or outside the cottage with Ralph, his father's last surviving friend.

'I'm glad we have a few minutes on our own, Peter.'

'Oh, yes.' Peter shuffled his feet. 'Is something wrong?'

'No, not with me, a few uncomfortable nights . . .'

'I'm sorry about that.'

'We're none of us getting any younger,' Ralph said bleakly.

'Joyce's all right, is she?' he asked Ralph, the protocol of The Round House based on circumnavigation: one asked one's question indirectly, news eventually got round. His father had written that history consisted of asking the right questions. For Peter, the history of the house was about avoiding being around when the answers were dealt out.

'Her psoriasis bothers her terribly,' Ralph said. Peter visualised it: Joyce showing Ralph her old bare arms, Ralph receiving letters from Kate – despite his better nature, he felt disgusted.

'What does the doctor say?'

'Just gives her more cream.'

'Is it working?'

'To my mind, illness is mental as much as physical,' Ralph began. Peter stopped listening, simply stood. 'The body is the barometer of the mind . . .'

'I really must go, Ralph, I've got rather a lot on.'

'I mustn't detain you. I think it's a good thing, going away. I certainly enjoyed my break last year, Spain . . .'

Peter skimmed his stick along the surface of a puddle. 'I must . . .'

'You know, you and I don't talk half enough . . .' The rooks going to roost were loud in the silence with which Peter greeted this last remark.

'Seeing you with that stick reminds me so much of your father . . .'

Always getting me in a corner, RF had written. *Only smokes a pipe because it takes an interminable time to clean and fill and smoke . . .*

They had coffee next morning in the conservatory before he left. 'Another yachtsman's gone missing,' Ralph announced, arriving with the paper. He had spruced himself up for the station, with a little bow tie and his hair parted neatly to the left; it was Friday, so perhaps he was going on somewhere else.

'Who?'

'One of the French, I think, part of the Crowhurst syndrome, don't you know,' elaborated Ralph. 'You remember, my dear' – he was addressing Nicola – 'all a ploy, of course, frightful. John Stonehouse was another one.'

'I'd forgotten all about Stonehouse.'

I hate this house and I hate this desultory conversation, Peter thought. Then why is it so difficult to go?

It was a rush to the station but then the train was its usual fourteen minutes late. Ralph helped him get the briefcases and the suitcase onto the platform.

'Thanks so much. I can manage these, please don't wait.'

'I'd like to.' Peter's heart dropped. The awful part of talking to Ralph was that there was never an end in sight, one could literally get stuck for hours; but the train was due in fourteen minutes. Peter suggested coffee; beyond the possibility of an act of a malevolent god, he considered himself safe. Ordering the drinks, he observed Ralph in the mirror behind the coffee bar. He did feel sorry, very sorry. 'Did my father say goodbye to you, Ralph?' he asked him without premeditation.

'Not as such, no. He came over, as I recall.' The sound of

his voice had a dulling effect; Peter made an effort to listen to what he said.

'It was March, you know, damn cold. I remember he read the riot act a bit – you know, about the cottage, about me. We had a pipe together . . .'

'Why did he read the riot act?'

'Oh you know, place in a mess, that sort of thing. He liked to think he kept me up to the mark. A good friend . . . I do remember that he seemed rather cross, and I remember thinking that was rather a good thing.'

'Why?'

'I thought he was better, more himself, looked better. He'd been awfully low, since Christmas; writing not going well, I suppose.' He paused to sugar his coffee.

'It had been like that for a long time?'

'Yes, I suppose it had. We didn't talk about it, you see. He didn't seem to want to talk. But him coming over like that, I thought he'd got some of his old form back, some of his old energy, fool that I was. I thought he was rallying a bit. I said as much later on to Joyce.'

'But he told you then, did he, that he was going away?'

'Yes, absolutely. He said he was going off for a few days and asked me to keep an eye on Joyce. The awful thing was that I was so dense, totally misread the situation, didn't sense a thing.'

'Didn't suspect?'

'Didn't suspect? I don't know, Peter, I really don't know.' *Nothing to beat the comfort of old friendships* . . . 'I thought about it a great deal.' He looked quizzically at Peter now: didn't suspect, don't know . . . 'It's a funny thing. We used to talk about it, suicide, years ago. If anyone was up for it, it was me; no children, you know. Then your father read a great deal, we talked about things. At that time he was very interested in Tolstoy, always said he'd read him and he did. Don't think his work was going well, he liked to read. I remember he actually read bits out to me about suicide, Tolstoy's diaries, we discussed it. To my mind it was something he was totally against. The point is that it wasn't

107

the sort of thing . . . quite the opposite . . . such a shock. I've thought about it a lot, gone over it in my mind.' Ralph fiddled with his frail bow tie. 'I sort of like to think, you know, that it was a mistake. But I don't know. I don't know whether I've rearranged things in my mind, my imagination, what have you, but in some ways it does fit in. Never thought much of the consequences, Richard, he could always act. I like to think, in your father's case, that if it wasn't a mistake, and I wish it was, that it wasn't what it usually is, wasn't despair. He was more angry that day, if you follow me, judging from the way he read the riot act that morning. I like to think it was a sort of rebellion or something, Richard making a sort of stand . . . What I'm saying is, I'm not putting this well and there isn't enough time, that it wasn't because of anything or anybody else – selfish, if you like, though that's a little hard – to my mind he was doing it for himself. In the end, he was himself.'

Ralph took his hand when the train came in. 'I wish we'd talked about it before,' he said. 'Seems ridiculous, can't talk about important issues, of course, you know what I mean . . .'

'I do.'

'Now take care, for God's sake, and enjoy yourself a bit.'

'I will.'

'And keep in touch.'

'Of course.'

They broke hands, lost touch. 'Oh, and Peter, take this.' He handed him his paper.

'Thanks.'

Given the opportunity, Ralph had gone on talking right to the very last moment. As the train pulled out, Peter watched Ralph walk away: that incongruous familiar figure, half male, half female, the wicker basket on his arm to collect Joyce's library books, the tight trousers (wherever did he buy his clothes?), the bow tie and the Guernsey sweater, tight wool over the sagging, ageing stomach. If there was a God, how could he square his love for man with the cards he'd dealt out to Ralph?

With the potent vision of Ralph's retreating figure in his mind, Peter opened the paper, which, being the *Telegraph*, had columns on the missing yachtsman back, middle and front. A journey from A, thought Peter as he read about it, Ralph's sticky circles of blue pen circling A Journey from A . . .

9

The world's my oyster. It was Monday lunchtime, but the place was already fairly full. Two men chatted quietly in a small fish restaurant near St James's. Talked about the Mulheimer Freiheit in which Felix was apparently 'up to his neck' involved, about the Neue Wilde School in Düsseldorf. 'It's not that the British don't buy art now,' Felix was saying, 'it's that they never did.' As he spoke, he dipped an elegant hand into a bowl of cashews and peanuts beside him on the table. Peter found himself quite mesmerised by the hand, gleaming and capable, precise as a dipping bird. 'Decco is a Berliner and the other guy's from New York; it's not that they complement one another but that they are doing the same thing. Like everything else,' again the fingers dipped, 'art is international now.'

Out of politeness, Peter could hardly disagree. He was wearing the suit Nicola had packed for him, the shirt she had folded, handkerchief in the pocket that sensibly she thought to include: it had taken him quite a little time to dress. He drank some vodka, nodded at Felix, was polite. In any case this was an essentially polite and civilised meeting, two men in a fish restaurant near St James's.

'Will you order now, sir?' The waitress addressed Peter, and why not? Her voice had Irish in it, a faint echo in this discreet room.

'Of course one has to go and get it. I like to think it's a bit like the old plant hunters, into the jungle for rare species. Everyone travels now, of course, even academics like yourself.' Felix was younger than Peter, he was enthusiastic and, as Peter had noticed that day of Audrey's funeral, the dipping hands gleamed.

'It sounds more fun than writing for a living.'

'Each to his own.'

Nothing belongs to me.

Felix ran his knife down a trout and removed the backbone with natural expertise, the neckbone connected to the backbone. 'How are you, Peter?' he asked.

'Well, I'm fine.'

'I was pleased to hear about the prize . . .'

They had discussed their business in general on the phone. Felix was good on the phone; so was Peter. Now they got down to the particulars.

'Which particular painting was it, Peter?'

'*Daring Miss Pears.*'

'Good, very good. Fine.'

'Have you exhibited her recently?'

'Not this year, no. I'd like to get something organised, next spring perhaps.'

'As far away as that.'

'I think so.'

Peter talked for the sake of talking, for the sake of concentrating on appropriate words. For two days he hadn't talked at all, but like riding a bicycle one didn't lose the knack.

'Is she quite successful?'

'Oh yes. We're delighted with her.' Felix made her sound like a four-year-old, a filly; Peter flicked a breadcrumb from his cuff. Two men, sober, suited, clean-cuffed, discreetly tied and parcelled, left the restaurant after an expensive, meagre lunch. They walked towards the gallery together through St James's, at one with their environment, urban, polished, sleek.

Felix left Peter with the German expressionist and his American counterpart. The atmosphere of the gallery reminded Peter of the Natural Food Store at Cherrington, sententious in some way, and empty. Felix dealt personally with one or two things.

'Do you wish to come down or would you prefer me to ask for the paintings to be brought up?'

'I'll come down.'

They descended to a heated basement. Kate's paintings were removed from their wrappings for Peter's close inspection. Felix insisted on hanging each of them, although Peter had already decided on *Miss Pears*, black, dark red, the patch of blue, the child with her mouth stuffed.

'I must say, I like it,' Felix said with warmth and more enthusiasm. 'She has what you writers call "her own voice".' He fiddled with the system of track lighting and dimmers, showing his wares to the best advantage. 'Getting your style early on can be a disadvantage; it's the cheese-grater syndrome,' he elaborated. 'There's a chap who did quite remarkably well at the beginning of the seventies. Painting domestic objects on a huge scale, isolated on the canvas – the cheese grater was the best known, made it look menacing, aggressive. You see, he had his style quite definitely. I exhibited him myself.' Felix seemed to have plenty of time to talk; Peter had time too. 'In any event, his painting changed, a different phase, less experimental than the first, he ceased to sell as well as before. Apparently a couple of years ago a dealer rang him and asked him for another cheese grater. That's the trap, you see – style early on.'

Salad King? Toss me another one, do . . .

'But you think she's good?'

'I think she's good.'

'I'll buy it,' Peter said. 'And of course you may have it back. I could loan it back at any time, should you wish to exhibit it again . . .'

'That's very kind.'

'Obviously I want the best for her.'

'We all do,' said Felix, recalling the state of Kate, the picture of distress as he'd driven her from The Round House back to London in his car.

Upstairs again, Peter wrote out a cheque for £1,750, replaced the cap securely on his pen. 'I shan't be able to take it with me unfortunately. Could you hold on to it for a day or two until I know exactly . . .'

'Certainly. If you wish, we could send it down Red Star.'

'Down? Oh no, not down. Not at the moment. I could let you know . . .'

'Fine.' Felix had completed the sale. As he'd said to Peter on the phone, he was off that evening to New York – so, 'I hope you enjoy New York,' Peter said.

'I always enjoy New York.' He walked his customer, his unexpected customer, to the door.

'There was something I wanted to ask you,' Peter said.

'Ask away.'

Peter looked at the grey-smoked glass of the door; it had silver threads running through it, to stop you cutting your arm, severing an artery.

'Are those burglar alarms?'

'Yes.' He shot Peter an odd look.

Peter collected himself. 'No. I meant to ask you during lunch.' Peter brought the card that Nicola had procured for him from his pocket. 'Do you know anything about this?'

'Not her best work.'

'No, but I'd rather like to have it, for Joyce. It's the fruit cage at The Round House.'

'Oh, I see.'

'You don't happen to know what happened to the original? It would be quite interesting to have, you see . . .'

'I think you're out of luck with this one. I think it already found a home.'

'You've got it?'

'No. Not me. Annabelle?' A girl who looked rather like Nicola moved across the carpet to where they stood. 'Chap called Clitheroe, wasn't it, who bought the cage? He's a collector. Look it up, Annabelle. In Surrey somewhere. Actually, between you and me, I think she gave it away, silly girl.'

'Phone, Felix.'

'Will you excuse me? Annabelle, pop Clitheroe's address in with Mr Fox's receipts, will you, and put him down for publicity. Look, Peter, good to see you, must fly, do excuse me, thanks for lunch.'

'Thank you.'

113

Some way away from the gallery, Peter leant against a wall and opened the envelope with the receipt. *James A. Clitheroe* (wee Jimmy?), Russell House, Netley Lane, Woking. He recognised that and wondered why. Russell House, Russell House? From the pages of the *Telegraph*, of course. It wasn't a house, Russell House, it wasn't a house at all; it was a home. Fastidiously he folded the paper, put it back. He felt conspicuous in London; he hid the paper in his pocket with the card. He didn't want anybody else to know. He felt conspicuous, the man on the hill fort wearing red. He walked, his arms close to his sides, down to the tube back to his hotel.

'Everything is international now.' Wherever he walked or went, you'd better believe it, Peter was on the spot. The world was well and truly mapped out for people like Peter. Someone in Ireland, someone else at Port Isaac, someone on the tube? A like mind, a congenial companion; above all, someone who knows you. Someone hiding round the corner, someone lurking by a tree. Of course the Isle of Wight had been an obvious choice . . .

Everything except escape is acceptable. Escape is as threatening as divorce once was; it questions the importance of what everybody else believes in – the corner boys, the tree peepers – it shakes the status quo. He must phone Hayward, and Jimmy Clitheroe and Kate's parents, mustn't he? Take the initative, spot them before they spotted him.

He'd panicked at Paddington on Friday. This was his Monday after a quiet and clean weekend. The train had thrummed with an insistent and familiar tune: 'Dem bones, dem bones, dem *dry* bones. Dem bones, dem bones, dem *dry* bones.' Travelling on to this rhythm, making it part of himself: 'The thigh bone connected to the knee bone, the knee bone connected to the leg bone . . .' Alel-lulia – at last – at last! 'Now hear de name of the Lord!' But more than the music had hit the buffers when they arrived. He moved along the platform with the other travellers, read as they read the huge lit billboard – HTV: YOUR STATION BACK HOME – but then he'd stood still, lost the music, a silly mistake: stand still

114

on Paddington station and you're suddenly in everybody's way. Peter formed an obstacle to the movement: 'Excuse me/ Do you mind!' Behind him was the billboard, the departures board, the rails snaking from the station to the west; in front more signs: BAKERLOO/DISTRICT/CIRCLE. Quite suddenly he was as confused as the Chinaman of Ig's little joke: 'Cabaret pronounced success.' Then Praed Street flashed its signs at him: ONE HOUR DRY CLEANING/EURO EXCHANGE/MECCA BOOKSELLERS/CRETE TRAVEL. Crete Travel — he'd stood and sweated in the street, his back against a window full of shoes; across the road he watched a flunky hailing taxis, a coach drew up outside a large hotel. He crossed the busy road, past the flunky, up the steps, through the revolving doors, into the Rendezvous Lounge of the Great Western Royal Hotel, into the brown and orange foyer, to sit down. The music had deserted him, he had no rhythm in his head. He ate a nut or two, ordered a drink, the Brunel bar deliciously and dimly lit. He picked up a leaflet from the table:*Das Great Western Royal Hotel ist international bekannt und eignet sich wegen* . . . whatever the function, experience has no substitute . . .' Peter, experiencing the eerie quiet of panic, read on. 'The Great Western Royal Hotel has the expertise and facilities to achieve success, *offre il locale ideale per visitare Londra sia per affari che per divertimento* . . .' Miles of vine and olives. He booked a room. 'Mr Brunel,' he told the registrar.

'That's a coincidence, sir. Isambard, is it?'

'Sorry.'

'Your first name, sir?'

'Peter.'

Das Great Western if you're going off the rails la gare is a better place than most, offre professional psychoanalysts, famed for its large deep baths. Peter had a bedroom with a large deep bath . . .

So, after his meeting with Felix, he returned to his bedroom and his bathroom, the briefcases belonging to his father, to Audrey and to Kate. He must take the initiative, mustn't he? Spot them before they spotted him. Sitting on the bed, he lifted the receiver from the phone.

The following morning he was up at dawn to get himself ready for the day. From his bathroom which looked out over Praed Street, he watched the world going to work; he was working well. Over the telephone he had already hired a car. 'A week, sir?' 'Just for the day. I'm going away and I have some business to attend to.' But you don't have to explain to Avis or Hertz, it's easy-peasy lemon squash, delivered to your hotel door. If you have your limbs removed, you may expect a phantom pain or two. Peter gazed through the double-glazed window and watched the world go to work; he felt no phantom pain. Nevertheless he couldn't be too careful; Russell House was a home.

He drove to Woking as Felix Switzer's business partner from Cork Street. He fiddled with the radio and at last got Jimmy Young. Jimmy was having a leading member of the animal rights campaign in the studio later in the prog. Till then it was bad music, bad music interspersed with worse music, running beneath weather reports, road reports, news. A home could mean all sorts of things. Why had Kate given her painting to a home? Gratitude, obligation? Kate aborting babies on the private patients' plan. Kate straightjacketed, led off. Kate in the company of crop-headed women masturbating beyond, beneath, a grille. Ken Russell wrote the screenplay, Jimmy Young had Abba singing Wagner, and he'd almost made himself late watching the people on Praed Street, the absorbing sanity of the ant hill. Please God allow me to concentrate on Jimmy Young. 'And with us in the studio today . . .' He turned right out of Woking, past the garden centre where Kate's father had calmed himself amongst the Levingtons and the leaf mould, took the drive through the pleasant gardens of Russell House where ordinary people (extras?) sat out in the May sunshine beyond the many-gabled Victorian house. Neither staff nor patients seemed in any way deranged, no different from the Praed Street shoppers, sandwich buyers. In through the porch, hats and scarves hanging on the pegs.

He was a little early. Mr Clitheroe had someone with him. Would Mr Fox like coffee, milk, sugar? Would Mr Fox like

116

to look at the paintings while he waited? 'My name's Anita, by the way.'

He shook hands with Anita and together they walked down the broad hall which was closely hung with paintings. Peter pretended a confidence he didn't feel, arranged his face to look rapt, intrigued, quizzical, Felixish. He looked in silence, for Anita had plenty of opinions of her own. Quite a few of the paintings were by patients, ex-patients. Clitheroe had a way with him for attracting tributes – in Kate's instance, better value than a piece of badly done raffia basketwork – some of them were rather obsessive, she said. 'Now here we are.' Ease deserted him; there hung the fruit cage; in Kate's manner, much larger than life. The size impressed him. He had thought of it as the size of the card he had in his pocket. The Round House fruit cage in a clinical corridor outside Woking, out of context, outside Woking – thank you, Kate. And in the corner of the fruit cage a little, previously undetected, patch of grey. Here I am tiny, and there it is clammy: yes, she got it right, full to suffocating – thank you, Kate! Betrayal on a large scale: I'm tiny, just a little patch of grey. He stared at the picture. Oh yes? Oh yes? There's me in the corner. It was a denial of him, this painting, a sort of triumph over him, a crowing: everything that had meant anything between them seemed broken beyond re-covery by a little, tell-tale, oh so teeny-weeny patch of grey. Kate as a hedge or shelter from the world outside, leave it out. Def-in-itely, leave it out. It pronounced Kate to be all right without him, not cowering but coping well, not begging for his favours or his help, as he had thought, had hoped? Not crop-headed; crowned. If *Miss Pears* was an exorcism of childhood, then this was an exorcism of him, of Joyce, of the house, of him. He didn't want to see wee Jimmy now. He wanted to go away and cry. How dare she, Kate Whittaker, take precedence like this, interfere with the memory – quiet Kate in a deckchair? Here was something that belonged to him, done by someone who evidently did not – *nothing belongs to me*. A thief in the night, she had burgled him, grey, grey flannel, the small boy trapped – well, thank you, Kate.

He would terrorise Smith's, he would buy them all; he had to have this painting to destroy. He wondered when she'd done it. She'd apparently done it here, but from memory or a photograph? Had she sketched it at the house? He remembered how he'd watched her draw: the hand, the talk he hadn't understood, about perspective and foreshortening — well, he'd been foreshortened now. He peered intently at the little boy in grey, not noticing Clitheroe creeping up beside him in the clingy silence of the corridor. 'Oh yes!' he said, furiously and out loud.

'Mr Fox?'

'Oh yes!'

'James Clitheroe.'

This wasn't the Kate, poor Kate, he'd imagined in the car. This was Katy fighting back, what Katy did afterwards; Kate fighting fit, fighting back. There was someone talking to him. He shook hands with Clitheroe, what a worm. He wanted the painting, he talked. 'I came in place of Felix Switzer, of Switzer's, he's in America, New York.' He talked quickly. Looking at the man, he felt it advisable not to leave any spaces. Clitheroe looked unpleasantly cool and Peter felt heated. Peter was maddened but he wasn't mad. He breathed deeply and went on talking — any pause, he felt, would be detected by this professional; like someone going to the police station to report a missing dog, Peter was anxious to avoid arrest. 'I'm extremely pleased with this one,' Clitheroe was saying, as if he'd mixed the paint, wielded the bloody brush. 'It's a wonderful picture, so full of life. We're very lucky to have it here.'

Peter nodded. Not for much longer, you toad.

'I was a little concerned that you were coming down to filch it from us.' This was a joke, apparently, and Clitheroe laughed. 'Filch' was a word Peter didn't much care for; the man looked as if he wouldn't give you a cold. Filch. Peter winced at the word. As a representative of Switzer's he felt considerably put out.

'One is naturally interested, in an artist of ours . . .' Did Clitheroe believe this pose? Instinctively, Peter felt he did not.

For all he knew, Kate had described him in minute detail to this man: '. . . and there he is, little boy stuck in the painting, still stuck now of course, still cringing . . .' His suit felt uncomfortable; involuntarily he squirmed.

'This one's positively not for sale,' Clitheroe continued, firm and pleasant, cleansing as a mud pack. 'The jewel in the crown, so to speak.' Again he laughed. 'Dreadful how these television metaphors impinge.' Now he stood back from the picture, his smile taking it and Peter in, the joys of ownership. 'I hope you'll join me for my mid-morning coffee, Mr Fox.'

'Thank you.'

'This way.'

Peter felt it necessary to put a spring in his step as he walked upstairs in front of Clitheroe: always watch your back – he felt his back to be eloquently transparent. He doubted he would ever get out of Woking now that he had come, but here he was going upstairs . . .

'The door on your left.'

Into the room and Clitheroe allowing the door to swing to, to close behind them.

'Actually,' he was saying as Peter took in the room, bland, Habitatish, clean, 'she left one or two other things here if you're interested.' Peter pretended to be interested; how horrible, how stifling, the room was.

'What a pleasant room,' he said.

'One can't work in a mess, can one? We were amazed, not to say delighted, when she donated the painting.' Peter noted the word 'donated', how complementary it was to 'filch'. 'I suppose in many ways we had come to think of it as ours by right.'

They sat down opposite one another, the desk between them. Peter beamed across an understanding smile.

'I felt,' Clitheroe went on, confident, self-satisfied, secure, 'that in some way we'd all taken a hand in it.' Anita came in with some coffee. 'You've met Anita.'

'Indeed.'

'Coffee is one thing not in short supply these days,' said Clitheroe, adopting an expression that spoke of shortages,

119

the price of electric-shock treatment, the poor standard of straitjacket manufacture? Peter took in the desk, the calendar, the executive game. He tried to imagine Kate sitting where he sat now.

'She must have been very happy here with you.'

'Oh, she was, I do think she was. Once she got to know us and our little ways. I think if any confirmation is needed, the painting says it all.'

'Absolutely,' said Peter.

Clitheroe pinged some saccharine into his cup, swivelled in his chair, checking the weather. They drank their cups of coffee, they smiled.

'I musn't take up any more of your time,' said Peter.

'Not at all. It's not often we receive a visit from such salubrious company.' This new oily word slid from his plaque-free teeth. 'I'm off to play golf actually.' He tapped the saccharine container with his finger. 'I suppose it's age,' he said. 'Golf doesn't seem to take it off. This is, after all, a desk job.'

'You must meet some very interesting people.' Peter plumbed the conversational depths.

'Everyone is interesting, Mr Fox.' The eyes pierced Peter; Peter withstood it. 'Now – if you'd like to see our other treasures.'

They left the room and went downstairs through a door marked CRAFT. Clitheroe unlocked a cupboard by the wall – keys on a key ring, just like Nesta – out came a portfolio. 'More of your Kate,' he said. 'I particularly love these cartoons, tremendous sense of humour, especially this one – I always think this ought to be on the prospectus.' He pointed to a picture of the garden just as Peter had seen it half an hour before. The garden perambulators had cards on their backs like ballroom dancers which bore the cool legend *mentally ill*. Peter's heart plummeted alarmingly.

'You find them disturbing?'

'I –'

'You shouldn't, you know.' And then, oh God, here it comes, thought Peter. Clitheroe took his arm. 'The fact is we are all involved. For an outsider, illness of the mind is always threatening, another country. There I go again! This, you see, is very much part of the world, our world, yours and mine.' He released Peter's arm. 'Now do come down and see us again, won't you, Mr Fox? Now that we've lost Kate, I've no one to bore about art.'

'It's been fascinating.'

'You're very kind.'

They stood together in the doorway. In the drive the girl Anita was fiddling beneath the bonnet of her car; Clitheroe ignored her. 'Things have changed so much in the private sector at least. I like to see myself, and others like me, across the country, as medical pioneers. What we offer here is rehabilitation to a world we freely admit is difficult. Rehabilitation through shared responsibility and confrontation.' Peter shivered at the word. He was in sight of his car; he just had to get across to it.

'Thank you so much. It's all been so interesting.'

'Not at all, Mr Fox. Come again.' The door closed behind him, locked?

Determinedly Peter sauntered towards his hired car. 'Having trouble?' he asked Anita in his relief at leaving Clitheroe behind him.

'It's flooded.'

'Oh dear.'

'I suppose you couldn't give me a lift in?'

'In?'

'To Woking.'

'If you like. If it's flooded, it'll dry out, I . . .'

'If you could.' Her smile was sticky. 'I'd be awfully grateful, I must get to the post office.'

'How will you get back?' Anita had a clutch of PO books in her hands. He wondered if she was running away.

'I'm off this afternoon,' she said, confusing him more, getting in beside him in the car. 'I'll probably bump into somebody.'

Peter drove distractedly, the possibility of bumping into something or somebody real to him. Anita chatted as they

121

drove the short distance to the town centre, showed him how to negotiate the one-way system.

'It's a nice day, isn't it?'

'Where can I drop you off?'

'Anywhere near the centre will do. It's nice to be out. Hasn't been much of a spring, has it really. I usually go to the pub on Wednesday.'

'Really.' Peter's hands were sweating: get into lane.

'I have lunch there, here it is. I come every Wednesday.'

'Oh, very nice.' Peter jerked to a halt, someone hooted. 'I'd join you,' he felt it necessary to say, 'but I have to be back in London.'

'Do you come to Woking much?'

'No. I don't. Well. Enjoy your lunch and thank you for showing me the painting.'

'My pleasure.' Again the sticky smile. 'So long then,' she said, obviously disappointed. Peter drove away, filtered out and up onto the uppermost slopes of the Safeway's multi-storey car park, where he burst into bitter little tears.

Back in his hotel room, in the big-bathroomed sanctuary of the GWRH, Peter put a seven-letter word to the tears in the car park: 'Goodbye'. An invitation to the dance *was* ironical if you were hopeless at the steps. No parent to sew the sequins, no partner to lead onto the floor; stand still and the silence becomes obvious.

Seven letters. Goodbye. He made an appointment to see Hayward, he telephoned the Whittakers at home.

'Hello, Mr Whittaker.'

Harold had rushed in from the garden. His wife Margaret, who dealt with the telephone, dealt with everything, was having her hair done. He picked up the receiver with a dirty hand, his trowel dropping wet earth at his feet. 'Yes?'

'Mr Whittaker. It's Peter Fox.'

Harold gripped the trowel hard; he'd made the handle himself – he would have made a lot of other things if he'd had grandchildren. 'Yes?'

'I'm in London. I wondered if I might come and see you?'

'From London?'

'Yes.'

'Oh.'

'I thought I might come down some time this week, Mr Whittaker. I know we haven't met, but –'

'When do you want to come?'

'Tomorrow, if that's convenient.'

'Could you hang on a moment, please.' Harold put down the receiver and the trowel, looked desperately about the empty tidy room: the parrot, the piano with its matching framed photographs of Kate and David, the children as children . . .

'I'm afraid tomorrow's a bit difficult for us.'

'The day after tomorrow.'

'Hang on.' Again he put the receiver down, studied the pattern of the carpet, the bit of trodden-in earth that would annoy his wife. 'All right,' he said guardedly. 'Before or after lunch?' Margaret worried about meals.

'After lunch, if that's convenient.'

'All right.' He replaced the receiver finally, considered the spilt earth.

Peter walked the last part of his journey to Covent Garden to keep his appointment with his publisher. He trod the pavement briskly, reminded himself that his publisher's place of work was, he knew it to be, a reassuring building. He knew it well, he knew it from when he'd gone there with his father as a child: the landings, the brown lino and the dust of ages which denied the high-tech shop front he now saw on Henrietta Street containing a Booker shortlisted author from last year. Nothing would have changed. The whole building was imbued with a sense of seriousness of purpose which one never for a moment suspected to be false. He smiled bravely as he waited in reception, flicking through the spring book lists for 1984. On the academic front a professor of sound reputation offered volume one of *The Art of Personification in Ancient Egypt*. More popular reading offered several additions to the Roper-Snow handbooks, including *Hand-*

Bell Tolling for the Beginner. There was something on mutual fingering that looked intriguing but turned out to be the work of a TV celebrity concerning the development of the pre-school child. Peter smiled bravely; he had come to say goodbye. Goodbye because, if you like, he was no longer *au fait* with the academic world and Salad King formed no part of it; goodbye because he had no conceivable use for a handbook that taught beginners how to peal; goodbye because he had no direct knowledge, and was now unlikely to have any, of the development of the pre-school child; goodbye because he didn't believe in gods Egyptian or otherwise; goodbye because the world was international now and he had no place to go; goodbye because Praed Street seemed extraordinary to him yet he knew that it was not . . . And why, he wondered as he sat there, did it take him so long every morning to get dressed? The outward appearance of normality, the clean cuffs, the pressed suit, pretence: 'Peter pronounced success.'

The coloured receptionist recognised him, said she was pleased to see him looking so dapper and so well. The despatch riders leaving parcels at her desk neither trod on his toes nor sniggered behind his back; and here came Hayward, last seen in speckled country tweed, now pinstriped, bounding down the staircase, greeting him like a long-lost friend.

Sweet of him to come in before he went away, everybody absolutely thrilled about the prize, deserved of course and certainly not before time. Anything else on the stocks? Well not to worry, not to worry at all. Take a break, a breather. Where was he going? Tuscany had been mentioned, absolutely marvellous, magnificent views, olive and vines . . . Actually while he was there, there were one or two books he might be interested in, a quote on the back, nothing too arduous. Now here was something his father had been interested in, *The Secular Society*, he might give that a go. 'Salad King speaks': seal of approval from prize-winning author – 'King's seal'? The talk ranged widely, more gossip than business. Hayward spoke of the Richard III society, hoped Peter wasn't too upset. Peter wasn't. That was sensible

They'd tried to save it but had been forced to admit that it had now, temporarily, collapsed. Well, history was fashion as much as anything else, wasn't it. Well, he needn't tell Peter that, teaching your grandmother to suck eggs. Hayward diagnosed the problem: hadn't been going long enough, what's fifteen years in terms of history, and once the endowment had dried up . . . Place had been taken over by some microwave firm apparently, he'd been in correspondence with Joyce about it, and she starting up a field-study centre in the cottage, what energy — it had to be admired at that age, didn't it, what drive. She'd done her bit trying to keep Richard III going, but the financial climate, well, even had a go at Ig's executors — and what good news about Nicola incidentally, great guns. Poor old Richard III, but rest assured, his time will come again, always another wave — they both noticed and passed over the awkward metaphor — wiser to suspend it for the time being; well, nothing else for it really. Perhaps Peter himself might eventually put up some money. Shame to see it go, good times there with RF — my goodness me, we had some nights. End of an era really, time passes, things change.

Good of you to come up to collect it all, especially as you're going away. Quite happy to send it down, but probably just as well, the post these days, the price, things get mislaid.

He stood up, Peter stood up.

Playing golf this afternoon, hardly played at all this spring, weather has been foul, playing with Barry, we play at Richmond — you know Barry, friend of Nicola's, small world. I'll get Judy to see to it all in reception for you. Nice to see you so much better, Peter. Well, no one looks good at a funeral, do they. Poor Audrey. Last time I saw you, wasn't it? End of an era. Only sorry I can't buy you lunch. If you'd given me a bit more notice, I could have arranged things better. Still, you Foxes always were an impulsive lot. Us businessmen a bit more tied of course; and we haven't had many fine afternoons this month — got to grab them when you can in this climate. Do you play at all? Ought to get together for a game when you come back. Now don't forget to send a card and keep in touch. . .

Judy left the switchboard to flicker while she went downstairs for the things. It was quiet in the reception area, lights flashed and winked on the silent machine, silent lights.

'I hope you can manage all this,' she said, groaning theatrically beneath the weight. 'Have you got a car?'

'I'll get a taxi.'

'I'll ring for one.' Silently she rang.

Peter looked at the things he hadn't expected to collect: what was left of the Richard III society, a couple of briefcases, a file or two, and really, why hadn't he anticipated it, Kate's painting, unwrapped, the painting RF had commissioned – Richard III ridiculous on a white horse.

The following day dawned bright and golfish. Beyond the bathroom window Peter observed the Londoner's habitual over-enthusiasm for warm weather: sandwich-buyers in cardigans rather than coats; a man parked on the pavement and entered Crete Travel, in a cap, sleeved T-shirt and jeans. Peter took more trouble to get dressed. The clothes covered up what was rotten inside. He knotted his tie firmly at his neck and wished that he was dead. Whittaker would probably kill him anyway, programme the parrot to peck. Well, Peter rather hoped he would. As he drove to Guildford, the weather changed to drizzle and then rain. 'What an awful spring.' Who cares? Whittaker might kill him, and yes, he rather hoped he would. He imagined Harold polishing up a twelve bore or perhaps something nastily functional and sawn off. Much to Kate's chagrin, her father had taken great delight in the Falklands war and by courtesy of the television had been with the assault forces virtually blow by blow. Talk of cold steel, close combat, bayonetting – all very much to his taste. Peter looked towards death and congratulated himself that it might now be in sight.

A flurry of activity preceded his arrival in the highly mortgageable crescent which contained the Whittaker home. Harold infuriated his wife by sweeping the already immaculate gravel paths of the equally immaculate garden and then insisted, he was adamant, on tidying up the garage before lunch. From dawn that morning he had been occupied: hoeing the shallot bed, securing tricky trails of clematis, planting out the lobelia, painfully stooping, big hands round frail seedlings, planting them one by one. Mrs Whittaker, observing all this, remained at her post within. If Harold did not lunch early, then lunch would not be cleared in time; she didn't want her kitchen ... at a time like this. In any case, Margaret had planned a simple, early tea. No matter what Peter had done or hadn't done, had precipitated, it was inconceivable that he should come all this way to see them and not have anything to eat. Not knowing as much as she would have liked about their visitor, she anticipated tastes of an esoteric kind, and for this reason she had baked an orange and walnut sponge, three layers, and a tray of cinnamon puffs – nothing, you understand, too sweet, but if Harold didn't come in for lunch ... She tracked him down in the garage.

'Give me that, Harold,' she tutted, taking the brush out of his hand. 'Now do come in now for your lunch.'

'I'm not hungry, Margaret.'

'You must eat.' How this state of affairs had arisen with her family – that she existed to feed them and they refused her even this – she did not know. Her role had dwindled to that of purveyor of unwanted meals; there had been plenty of tears, which only the parrot had observed.

In silence they ate: tinned soup with croutons from the freezer garnished with Harold's early chives. Both were upset but neither, in the terminology of Miss Poppleberg, were able to vocalise how they felt. Like the parrot, they ate calling to one another in disjointed words and phrases that were something less than human conversation.

'Come on,' she hurried him. 'Take your coffee.'

'Can't I sit down?'

'Aren't you going to change?'

'No.'

'Harold!'

'Are you changing?'

'Of course I'm changing.'

127

They changed together in the cold bedroom, the night storage heaters firmly off. Margaret did her face and dabbed her neck and wrists with scent, put on her favourite pair of 'heels'. Too early they sat downstairs and waited for Peter to arrive. The house, tidied earlier, was perfect. Harold read the *Express*, Margaret moved ornaments and straightened the fringes of the standard lamp; neither of them spoke.

And yet they both found him charming, very nice and very polite. Older than they'd expected, rather shy, very nicely mannered, different from his father, more reserved.

'It's nice to meet you,' Margaret said.

'Yes, I thought we ought to meet.' But why? he wondered as he said it. And why? they wondered as he spoke. The room was perfectly neat: a slippery amber covering on the easy chairs, the parrot's cage in which the bird appeared to sleep. They looked at the garden through the windows; from the crescent came the sounds of children, slinging satchels, kicking at tins, happy in the brief time before one mutual fingering stage merges with another, coming home from school. The sitting room was divided from the kitchen by a waist-high stone partition. From where Peter now stood he could read the digital kitchen clock: 3.42 p.m.

'I gather Kate's settled in Newlyn. Do you hear from her at all?'

'My wife writes regularly.'

'Oh.' Peter cleared his throat. The parrot looked up and round at him. He tried again. 'I bought a painting of hers just the other day, from the Switzer gallery.'

'That's nice.'

'Yes.' Peter felt desperate, felt the parrot's glance. 'I thought it would be nice, nice to have one, a piece of her work. He looked about the room where no paintings hung. 'Did she finish her commission all right, Janet and Jim?'

'She always finishes what she starts,' said Harold, cold steel in his eye. He was all dressed up and he couldn't see the point of it at all. He would have to change back into his gardening clothes; he noticed that outside the rain had stopped.

'My husband said you were going away?' They all sat down together like musical chairs. Peter double-crossed his legs. 'Anywhere nice?'

Peter cleared his throat, the parrot mimicked him. 'I hadn't decided exactly,' he said. 'It's quite difficult to decide.'

Money had made the decisions for the Whittakers. 'It must be nice to have the choices you have,' Harold got in quickly, steel in his voice. Margaret looked wistful for a moment, the parrot coughed again.

'Will you have some tea?'

'I'd love some, that would be nice.' Nice?

Margaret went through to the kitchen, the top half of her body in sight above the stone partition which was hung, overhung, with fronds from varied, variegated plants.

'Kate said you were a keen gardener?'

Harold nodded. The parrot stared rudely at Peter and Peter began to sweat.

'Mr Whittaker, one of the things I wondered, something I wanted to ask . . . I came across a picture of Kate's, a card. I'm not explaining this very well, and Felix, that's the owner of the gallery, Feliz Switzer, suggested I track down the original, track it down because the picture is connected with The Round House –'

Harold nodded unhelpfully again.

'I went to the home in Woking, Russell House.'

'Oh yes.'

'I wasn't sure, I couldn't help wondering, in what capacity she had stayed there.' Peter, embarrassed as much by the hostility of the parrot as his host's rude manner, twiddled anxiously with his tie. 'I was rather upset, but then, perhaps I shouldn't have been. The point is I thought she might have been a patient there.' He looked at Harold but Harold didn't budge. 'After she left us at The Round House, the way she left us, quite suddenly, and then I knew about her brother, your son . . . After my aunt died, she was upset. I simply wondered, putting two and two together . . .' An abortion or a breakdown? he should have asked Harold. Tell me, you miserable old sod!

'She did some teaching there. Isn't that right, Margaret?'

'Pardon me?' Margaret came in with a laden tray. Harold sat stolid. The parrot observed. Peter uncrossed his legs, offered to help her; a table was slid out from a nest of tables.

'Mr Fox wants to know about Russell House,' repeated Harold.

'I never went there myself, I'm afraid. Harold visited; very nice, considering. I know I shouldn't say so but I don't like those places, makes me upset.'

'Quite.'

There was a silence as Margaret removed the tea cosy, poured the tea, handed round the side plates.

'Very brave of Kate to tackle it, to teach there.'

'Yes, we're very proud.'

They were lying. Were they lying? Would they lie about that sort of thing? Were nerves a stigma in this house? Most probably they were. 'I'm glad I asked you. I wouldn't like to have gone away without knowing, leaving any loose ends. I was very fond of Kate.'

'You were responsible for her,' Harold said, 'when she was staying down with you.'

'Now Harold,' warned Margaret.

'Now Harold,' the parrot said.

'Any decent man is responsible,' said Harold, putting down his plate. Harold had been responsible. To Harold, wife, children, garden and garage – primarily obligations.

'Mr Clitheroe said there was no one to blame, Harold. These things happen. A combination of circumstances.' Margaret turned away from Harold and towards her uncomfortable guest. 'Our son David . . .' The sentence hung in the air. Harold blushed.

'I don't want to bring all this up again for you. I'm sorry,' Peter said. 'Perhaps I shouldn't have come.'

'He's out now,' said Margaret calmly.

'Done his penance.' Harold's voice had fallen from steel to ordinary, everyday, disappointed, gruff.

'Both our children have had their ups and downs,' said Margaret.

'We haven't any grandchildren. Just the garden,' Harold said.

'Look, I'm sorry.' Peter didn't know what he was sorry for, but sorry he really was, sorry for coming, sorry for stirring things up. It occurred to him that Margaret and Harold were not in the habit of speaking openly to strangers, and why should they be, why should they? 'Well,' he said. 'Kate is a great success with her painting, I gather.'

'She always had a talent for it.'

Peter ate a biscuit. The parrot made a crunching noise. Peter looked firmly about the tidy room, the photographs on the closed piano. 'It's very pleasant here,' he said, using a lukewarm word which complemented the sun now shining on the wet garden.

'We're happy with it.'

'If you'll excuse me' – Harold got up – 'I'd like to get out while it's dry.'

'I do apologise for Harold,' Margaret said after he'd gone.

'Please don't. I'm the one who should apologise.'

'You've said your piece; it's finished now.'

The parrot had got bored with them and closed his eyes on Peter and Margaret, sitting in silence now, 4.12 p.m.

'Have another cup; it's still warm.'

'May I smoke?' He offered her the packet.

She hesitated for a moment. 'Thank you, I will.' She leant towards him for a light and he tried to find Kate in her, in this neat, fixed, still-attractive, loyal woman.

'It hit Harold very hard. He did all the visiting, you see, and she wasn't herself just then. Well, really she's had a history of it, depressions; so, you see, it's not really your fault. But it was very distressing for us, coming after David. She was only there a little time, four or five weeks; she needed a bit of a rest.'

'She's all right now?'

'Couldn't be better. She loves Newlyn and we've both been down to visit. Your family have been very good to Kate.'

131

'Except me.'

'It's a lovely spot, Newlyn,' she said, ignoring this. 'Have you seen it?'

'Yes, I took Kate down there after my aunt died.'

'She was ever so fond of you, you know.'

'I was fond of her.'

'I think it's a great pity how young people don't seem to be able to make a go of things these days,' Margaret said, delicately extinguishing her cigarette. 'The trouble is that you all expect too much.'

Peter cleared his throat again. 'I mentioned the painting. Well, I also have another one, one my father commissioned, you may remember . . .'

'I remember your father. I was saying to Harold just the other day, we wondered if he ever got his bird.'

'A parrot?' Peter shook his head.

'I'll tell Harold.' She smiled. 'He was a nice man, your father, but I said to Harold at the time he was more interested in the woman, Miss Poppleberg, than he ever was in birds. Did he get to meet her?'

'I don't think so. Did you?'

'No. It's Harold's interest really; he fills in the forms for her. Between you and me, it's the forms that interest him. He's been dealing with forms all his working life, quite lost without them.' She gave a tired smile. 'Sorry, you were saying about the picture?'

'I've got it in the back of the car; it's of Richard III.'

'Oh yes.'

I wondered whether you wanted it, on loan? The society has closed down.'

'Oh, well, I don't really know. It's very nice of you, but we don't really have the space for Kate's things here, much as we'd like to. Why don't you keep it, make a pair?'

'If you're happy with that arrangement.'

'Oh yes I think so.'

Peter stood up, unwound his legs, felt shaky – perhaps Harold had spiked the tea? He was outside now in working gear, digging vigorously at the bottom of the garden. To the

132

east the sky was clouding up again. Looking about the room, he saw how inappropriate Kate's paintings were to her background. 'This must be them,' he said, looking at the matching framed photographs: two children, white socks, polished shoes, brushed straight hair, little coats with velvet collars. He turned towards Margaret. 'Thank you so much, Mrs Whittaker.'

'Margaret, please.'

'Thank you, Margaret. Thank you for the chat and the splendid tea. I did want to sort things out before I went.'

'I'll say just one thing,' said Margaret firmly. 'The grass isn't greener on the other side, young man. David was all for travel and it didn't get him very far. You don't get away by going away. We were fond of your father, Harold and I, very fond, he was very good to Kate. You ought to be settling down at your time of life, not up and going away. He was very proud of you, your father, really proud, and I'm sure he wouldn't like to think of you swanning off. I'm lecturing you and I shouldn't but, like you, I want to say my piece. I don't like to see young people making mistakes. I've seen too much of it, believe me.'

Peter was touched, he shook her hand. 'I'd like to say goodbye to Harold,' he said. He went out into the garden, put his hand out to the man, moved by Margaret, who watched him from the window, unhappy about her perceptions of him, upset by the photographs on the piano. The man with the grubby hand took his clean one. 'Thank you very much for seeing me, Mr Whittaker, I'm very grateful.'

'Right.' The man's brow furrowed as a ball hurtled over the wooden fencing from next door, bounced off his clematis orientalis and landed on the perfectly mowed lawn. Peter picked the ball up and threw it back.

'Blighters,' said Harold. 'Little Bs!'

10

Peter woke up, came to, that's how he felt, on the hard shoulder of the A23I outside Guildford; his mind dawdled, his legs felt uncomfortably cramped. He got out of the car, glad for a breath of fresh air. Somewhat confused, he peed in the hedge, stamped the sleep out of his feet, noted the rush of passing traffic, peered through the window of the unfamiliar hired car at the dashboard to take in the time: 7.21 p.m. His mind cleared then clouded once more. *Miss Pears* and *Richard III* shared the boot of the car with his father's briefcases, and his father had been talking to him in a dream. Something inconsequential – *Every tessera was perfect, the shale was taken from the beach at Kimmeridge in Dorset.*

Peter thought of Kimmeridge, the folly tower, what had it been about . . . and then, that's it, his father had knelt down and kissed the mosaic floor. Peter could see his face very clearly, an expression of bliss almost, uncomplicated joy, as if nothing else in his life mattered but the perfection of this floor. *Every tessera was perfect.*

Where am I? Peter got back into the car, lit a cigarette that didn't taste too good, studied the map: Bagshot, Frimley, Worplesden, Normandy? Kimmeridge? *The Cruel Sea* on a well-dusted low book shelf at the Whittakers' house in the crescent – *The Cruel Sea, The Battle for Normandy, They Came Back, Pearl Harbor* – the shelf in that room with the closed piano, the novels of Pearl S. Buck. And yet his father was still with him after the dream; he could clearly see the expression of joy on his face. His father was with him and together they bounced off the hard shoulder and back onto the road. In Shalford he managed to find a phone:

134

'May I speak to Mr Clitheroe please?'

'Sorry. Mr Clitheroe's on holiday this week. Is there anyone else you'd like to speak to?'

What was her name? 'Anita?'

'Just a moment, I'll see if I can find her for you.'

Peter imagined briefly the corridor, the porch, the hats and coats.

'Hello?'

'Hello. Anita. This is Peter Fox. We met when I visited Mr Clitheroe last week.'

'Oh hello.' Her voice was sticky warm. 'What can I do for you then?'

'Well, it's a bit difficult really. I wanted to speak to Mr Clitheroe.'

'He's away on holiday at the moment.'

'Yes, I gathered.' Peter hesitated.

'Can I help at all?'

'Thank you, I don't know. I should have phoned earlier. I'm afraid this is all a bit last minute. Miss Whittaker is having an exhibition, down in Cornwall, in Newlyn, at the Orion. I'm on my way there now. I wrote to Mr Clitheroe, he probably didn't have time to see to it before he went away, the letter's probably on his desk.'

'Do you want me to run up and . . .'

'No. Look, don't bother. The point is, she, Miss Whittaker, expressed a wish to hang *The Fruit Cage* and some of the sketches.'

'Oh.'

'I did write but it obviously got snowed under . . .'

'Oh well, I can't see that he'd mind; you want to come over and get it, do you?'

'Yes. I did wonder if I might. I'm in the area actually, well more or less. The thing is . . .' The phone at this point began to whirr and click. Peter slotted in a further couple of coins.

'Hello?'

'Still there.'

'You'd be happy to take the responsibility?'

'Oh yes.'

'Okay. Well, I could be with you in half an hour. You're sure it's not too late?'

'Only too glad to help,' she said. He imagined her lank brown hair. 'I'll get everything ready for you then.'

'Thanks, that's very kind.'

Perhaps it was Clitheroe's absence that evening which gave Russell House its air of dangerous looseness, of laisser faire. There were no patients to be seen, yet it was barely after 8.00 p.m. Waiting at the door, he imagined the patients roosting in their rooms, the tapes of their straightjackets hanging loose like trails from hooded birds. The door was opened by a young male nurse who took him down the corridor to a small sitting room in which Anita sat. She got up at their knock and came into the corridor. The painting had already been removed. With Anita beside him, he carried it back down the corridor, through the hall door and out to the car.

'So kind of you to see me at this late hour.'

'Glad to see anyone in this dump.' Had she been drinking?

'You're in charge, are you?'

'More or less.'

He opened the boot.

'Oh, you've got some others for her, I see. Big, aren't they?' He closed and locked the boot. Now what? 'Thank you so much. Right. Well, I ought to make a move . . .' Anita looked disappointed, Peter saw the noose and put his head in it. 'I'm only sorry I didn't get a chance to buy you a drink last time.'

'That's all right.' She slurred the word; he was sure that she was drunk.

'I imagine that you like to get out.'

'Why don't you come in and have a drink with me,' she suggested.

'Oh yes, I will, very nice.' Peter was behaving like a fool. He checked the boot again, locked the driver's door of the car, went back through the house with the keys in his hand; what had seemed to him quiet when he entered just now was actually restless, coughs and noises off, stage left and right, into the little private sitting room. Clitheroe's? Anita's? A paperback was open face-down on the table, a pair of slippers together on the sofa.

'Hard on the feet?'

'Hard on the head, more like!' Anita poured him a glass of Californian red wine from a carafe. 'Here's to you, then. Now sit down here next to me.' She flicked the slippers to the floor. He settled bitterly in the corner. Anita lit a long-length Peter Stuyvesant cigarette. 'Are you driving down tonight then?'

'Part of the way.'

'It's a long drive.'

'Yes.'

'When does the exhibition start?'

'Wednesday,' said Peter off the top of his head.

'Plenty of time then.'

Peter tried hard to concentrate on what she was saying. 'Yes, well, not really. It's all . . . got to be hung and then there are private views, press shows.' He drew a careful breath. 'Mr Clitheroe would have enjoyed it. He's very interested in painting, isn't he?'

'Yes.' But Anita wasn't interested in Clitheroe. 'Do you know Katherine well?'

'No. No, I don't. I only know her professionally. I was actually with her parents just this afternoon, collecting something.' A flea in the ear, he thought. 'I expect you met her parents?'

'Not the mother. I remember him.'

'Harold,' said Peter, thinking about the man. 'A keen gardener.'

'That's the one. He used to combine visits with trips to the garden centre. For some reason that irritated her. I'm not interested in gardening myself.' Her pale stockings were dark, damp-looking at the toe and heel, looked sweaty. 'So you're not going far tonight then?' Anita veered towards a proposition. The idea appalled him, and then his vanity appalled him too.

'Back to the West Country,' he said vaguely.

Anita had finished her drink and poured herself another one. 'Can I top you up?'

'No, thanks.'

'She lived there, you know, the West Country, before she came to us, until some bastard fucked her up.'

'Really.'

'Usual thing,' said Anita. Peter put his hands round his glass to steady them, his keys were on the side table by the door. 'I suppose you know her from way back, then?'

'No. As I said I know her professionally. My colleague might have visited her, Mr Switzer. He's away at the moment in the States.'

'You knew about her breakdown then?'

'Vaguely we knew, we knew she had been –' Peter searched for a phrase and found one of Joyce's. 'Overworking. Our artists,' he prattled on, anxious to avoid details of Kate's breakdown. 'We take a paternalistic attitude, a vested interest in keeping them on the rails.' He laughed weakly. Anita expected cynicism. 'We're not a charity of course.'

'Nor are we.'

'Obviously.' He stood up, 'I'm sorry, but I ought to be getting on now.'

'Oh, do stay, have another drink. It's nice to chat.'

'I'd love to but I've got a long way to drive. Drink and drive; it's not a very nice night.'

'Well, have some coffee then before you go.'

'Okay.' Easily defeated he sat down. Miserably he waited for the coffee – a drink would have been quicker. Was he going to get away with this or not? What did Anita know?

'She had a thing about eggs.'

'Who did?'

'Katherine Whittaker.'

'Really?'

'It was ever so odd, never quite got to the bottom of that one.'

'Is that what you have to do, get to the bottom of things?' He looked at her bottom, hated himself some more.

'In a way. Mr Clitheroe is a context man, a bit of a

138

pioneer really. He likes to tease out all the strands.'

'Yes, he mentioned . . .'

'If you get right to the bottom of things, it sort of stops them recurring, stops the rot.'

This sounded basic to Peter rather than pioneering. 'It sounds painful,' he commented.

'The whole thing's painful, isn't it?'

'Of course, yes. You must find it distressing, depressing?'

'It's a job, isn't it.' He wondered whether she had any qualifications. 'Jobs are hard to come by. I get on with Clitheroe, so I'm all right.'

'I see.'

'They're suffering from life, he says.'

'I'll drink to that.' At last she gave him the coffee. He stood up to take it from her and picked up his keys from the table by the door. My kingdom for a Chinese dog, he thought. I've got to get on now.

Anita had settled once more on the sofa. 'He saw the egg thing as a sign of new life, new birth, if you follow me. She wouldn't give an inch when she first came here. He said our job was to re-confront her with her talent, give her back her confidence and that. He kept trying to make her draw, nothing doing. She had this egg, a solid one, the sort you put under hens to make them go broody, or when they are broody, something like that, delph eggs. I've got it here somewhere, perhaps she'd like it back. Here it is. Look.' She leant behind her and took the egg from a large ashtray. Again Peter wondered whose sitting room it was, with its cona machine, its drinks cabinet. Anita had the egg that Peter had saved from Audrey's handbag after her death, the egg wrapped in tissue, marked *For Kate*. 'She rolled this thing round and round,' Anita was saying. 'Palm to palm.' She mimicked the actions as she described them. 'Hour after hour. It seemed a comfort. I wanted to take it off her, got on my nerves, but Clitheroe said I'd better not. Anyway in the end she upped and left it here, funny really.'

'Perhaps she no longer had a need for it,' said Peter, thinking of the painting and that patch of grey.

'That's just what he said, she'd grown out of it. Here, take it if you want it.'

It seemed expedient to take it and to go. Peter put it quickly into his pocket, felt his pocket sag. 'I really must go. I'm late as it is. You've been more than helpful.'

'All in a day's work.'

'Well, thank you.' She slipped into her slippers and walked out of the sitting room and back – allelulia – and, at last, along the corridor and to freedom and the front door.

'I expect I'll see you when I return the painting.'

'Right.' She staggered slightly in the hallway.

'When exactly is Mr Clitheroe due back?'

'The fourteenth.'

'Fine, well, I'll see he has a letter on his desk.'

'Right.'

'Goodbye then, thank you.'

'Remember me to Katherine, won't you? Tell her I'm glad it all turned out all right.'

Peter almost ran to his car, he couldn't get the key into the ignition fast enough, said what he'd come to say. 'Goodbye.'

11

Peter got rid of the hired car and bought himself a pram, an Oxfam, baby-carriage of a pram. A flunky stood by it while Peter backed out of the GWRH, carried everything that belonged/didn't belong to him, out through the hotel's revolving doors. *Richard III* and the tracing of the Birdlip mirror, *Daring Miss Pears* and the letters from Audrey to RFF, the Cretan Diary, Kate's delph egg, *The Journey from A*, the briefcases, Clitheroe's *Fruit Cage*: disparate items which had homogeneity to him, which he laid, with some reverence, in the bottom of the pram. He walked it along Praed Street a little, then on to the station, where he positioned himself on a bench with the rail bar behind him, put the brake on the pram the way they'd shown him in the shop. It was sixish, Friday night, busy.

None of the windows in the hotel had faced the station, no loudspeaker station announcements had permeated the muffled sanctuary of the massive lounges, the brown and orange carpeted calm which celebrated the memory of Isambard Kingdom Brunel. The station was new to Peter, who had not had time to notice it in the eerie panic just a week before, to Peter, who previously had always travelled everywhere by car. Overwhelmed, overstimulated, he simply sat, picked out the pigeons who pecked around about his feet, the pigeons who, once one becomes familiar with them, can be identified one from the other by their considerably varied plumage coupled with the extent of the mutilation of their feet. 'Blinkered', Kate had called him, in those long-gone days of the car, but Peter now picked out the individual from the crowd. The tramps were like the pigeons, this one with a big and bandaged foot, this child-like one wearing a waisted coat, this old man with a face dented like a ring doughnut, talking to the girl in pink beside him, talking without the benefit of teeth. He had felt he was drowning in London and that no one noticed or knew, but seeing it at ground level, by the rail bar, on the bench, altered his impression of the place. London refused to be shocked into sentiment; he might drown in it, but they wouldn't gloat or hold his head down, push him in. His father had been human, not a paragon or a pig. Kate was not a harridan because she failed him as a hedge.

All was quiet and peaceful, snuggled, cosy in the battered pram: gently he leant over it, opened the briefcase Hayward had given him, disposed of a shaving brush he found in the bottom and a sheaf of blank paper on a clip, glanced at an old agenda of his father's historical society and before disposing of it too, read what was written in long hand on the back:

Have decided to cut down on the drink, can do bill anyway, this bloody town. Even Cobbett had a thing against it, not surprised. Oddness levelled out, down to the pay the bills looking distinctly odd next time, why not . . . I remember years ago with Clem in Bedford Place, there was a chap who walked backwards and a woman with a beard who ran the ironmongers, sold paraffin. Someone else who pushed a pram full of mongrel dogs. Can't quite remember, getting to be a problem this, time telescoping, imagination and memory, nostalgia, sentimentality, synthesis and bloody myth. Not seen Audrey since I went down with Kate, won't do it again, can't now. Gone barmy of course, like the rest of us, too old to be any damn good. An advanced copy of P's latest from H, more than adequate, I think. Bedford Place, not the same at all. Down there just the other day with Joyce, rabbiting on about something or other, the garden, God knows, leant against the cold counter in the supermarket and felt quite sick, head swimming, not hangover, just despair. Frisby's, Oliver's, Dewhurst's, W.H. bloody Smith's, Boot's the Chemist; do other people feel this and not say so, does Joyce feel anything at all? Sections of crazed bricks round the new library that can no longer afford to buy any books, felt quite crazed just looking at them. Joyce had some idea about glazing fruit, flowers, something, sent me out for ascorbic acid, something. Couldn't get it of course. Thought I might take a massive dose of something, well thought crossed my mind; Boot's prescription counter won't serve during lunch. Getting tired and weakly. Go out for a walk and have to sit down when I know I'm out of sight. Difficult house The Round House, clear views out. V. amused by Ig's book, now in 2nd edition! Much better picture of me than I could have done myself. Wrote to say so at the time. He's dying, they all are. Saw Gombrich on the box, said he'd made a lot of new friends, at 96, can you credit it? Can you imagine, bothering? Really v. amused by Ig. Tried to discuss it with Ralph, not interested, still hopping about on one leg, silly bugger, like to discuss it with someone, that's all, everyone dying off.

Had a beer in Cherrington, tried to get into conversation with Lapwell, the estate agent, but he backed off. Felt I wanted to know how other people feel but no one's talking, can't tell, won't tell. Is place important? Never was to me up to now. It was people; now there are no people and I hate this place, living here. Hate The bloody Round House, knew I would, was happier living with money problems in my cottages, not really delighted to be living here in direct evidence of our great history. Funny how it goes, history paying me back. Just find it a bit depressing, ashes to ashes, all that. Those years with Clem, this place brings it back of course, Audrey, failure, more than sorry for that. Don't have to worry about money now, quite lost without it, concentrates the mind, don't have to worry, not allowed to worry, 'tires me', so I'm told. Not expected, allowed to worry about Peter, he doesn't want me to, so he says. Diet of fresh food and veg and fruit from the cage, like being in a bloody home, that's what's wrong with it, not a house but a home, capital H Home. A home in which I'm supposed to take it easy, not 'overtire' myself with writing. Nothing I want to say anyway or write. Bloodaxe caught my imagination, briefly, a big man, c.f. A.S. Chron. Read War and Peace, *always said I would when I got the time. Napoleon like Ig: 'A mind unaware of its own limitations, believing sincerely in its own impostures, running always to rhetoric'. Went to the funeral. Joyce fussed, in the end both went. No Peter, pretty awful all round. One loves one's friends for their failures. Too much to put on his gravestone, more's the pity. Reading biog of Tolstoy plus diaries and letters, intrigued but not always impressed. 'A life characterised by seeking.' Barking up the wrong tree but still barking, at least he had the energy to bark. Tolstoy got pretty depressed, younger than me, fifty odd. I staved it off for longer. 'I feel as if the rug were pulled from under my feet.' I feel, living here, as if the floors have been retiled, crazy paving, slippery and hard for an old boy to get a grip, 'worn treads'. Old age is outrageous, undignified, too much at the mercy of everybody else, I shall never get used to it, nor will they. Slippery floors, frightened of ending up on my back, legs in the air. 'You will never leave this city.' This is almost the end and it doesn't matter. Poor Ig, poor Tolstoy. What shall I have written on the stone, 'walked a lot, also ran'? Bought glycerine for Joyce, she needs to preserve eveything including me, exhausting. Gave me a book on Churchill's painting, hobbies of the great, good God, never went much for him. Nevertheless if I can't bark I'll trace, taken up tracing, stuff from the library van, Joyce getting me picture books, what she decides I want. Actually, the Birdlip mirror, it's hard I think to imagine anything more beautiful, more simple, you see anew when you're tracing. 'In praise of tracing' – RFF! I saw how the curves and spirals on the mirror-back were similar to the circles of hill forts from the air. It's the use of both which breaks the spirit, breaks the heart. I did the mirror and a particularly beautiful pair of harness mounts from Sutton Hoo, enjoyed it immensely, immensely satisfying and none of the gruelling deferred gratification of digging or book writing, finished in an afternoon. Go to the van to get my books, order them up, pensioner's rights, let the buggers pay. Suppose I'm like the rest of them off in their zimmers to buy or swap puzzles, the puzzle club, in praise of tracing, good grief. Still v. relaxing tracing, and effective too, makes me think of Peter, makes me sad. Have to admit hopes for one's children, liked him to have stepped beyond history, been a bit more daring, more creative. He might not understand that, I suppose. My notes are full of supposing, the supposing months or is it going to be years? 'For an active man dying is awfully passive' – damn right. 'Sometimes it occurs to me to go far away from it all' – it occurs to me as well. Dislocation is what I feel, life in the town, life out of it. Peter traces rather than paints but I detect a chink of light, might come good, shan't be around to see it.*

Constantly trying to avoid Ralph, really too much. He's a lonely old boy, it oozes from him, it seeps out, more than I can take at the moment – take on board, I think, is the expression. Then of course he makes himself ridiculous with all and sundry, assuaging his loneliness, giving presents he can ill afford, surely it can't still be sex? Ralph has got worse if anything; perhaps I'm hard on him, perhaps it's me. Not his homosexuality but his need for people, any people, for company, for conversation about anything, he'll talk about anything. I've tried with him, absolutely anything will do. We all need someone to talk to, he says, cornering me in the garden, by the fire, in the conservatory, lighting up that infernal pipe, 'having a quiet pipe together', him talking, what have you. Not sure we do all need someone to talk to. I don't want anyone to talk to. I'd like to lay my head down in Audrey's lap, bony old good lap. Too much emphasis on talk these days, discussion, negotiation, arbitration, television chat, too much noise, empty vessels, people talking out of books. People talking for the sake of it, nothing achieved except a temporary respite from loneliness, loneliness assuaged pro tem. Do know that I shan't stand by much longer, leave everything to Peter and Joyce, Ralph can keep the cottage, won't be a selfish act. Riders to the sea. Not selfish, rational. Letter and bumph from Miss Poppleberg today, now she's a good girl. Poppleberg and the parrot, fruitless research, never met her, sounds dotty, but such enthusiasm, I like it. Refreshing. Love her language, her absolutely serious

dissertations about the vocalisations of the African grey, com-
puterised prognostications. Language should change, all for
that, shows it still alive. Should get Ralph a parrot, specify in
my will. Live for years apparently, like tortoise. She says my
handwriting is marvellous 'for a gentleman of my years', over
eighty, makes me roar with laughter. Enthusiasm leaps
beneath the jargonising. What one lacks at my age is mental
energy to fire enthusiasm. Enthusiasm is the oil for old
bodies, I have virtually stopped secreting it, I'm drying up.
Good days when I write to Poppleberg, trace or do a bit on
Bloodaxe. Joyce asks me when I expect to be finished, is she
mad? I don't intend to finish, that would be ridiculous now
that I'm interested. Finish and be finished but she wouldn't
understand that. She's besotted by the news, Torville &
Dean, Bread and circuses, that wretched Bolero over and
over again ...

And music played. Peter hadn't noticed as he read. The girl in
pink had left now and the man with the ring-doughnut face
had been joined by another in a pork-pie hat. The two old
boys, a familiar sight on Friday nights at Paddington station,
the pensioners who collected the takings, whose presence
together signalled the imminent arrival of the band. A
crescent of chairs, three deep, beers brought out, music
stands erected, battered odd-shaped cases for clarinet, and
suzaphone, and sax. In a dream he watched the small, tight,
almost robotic movements of the middle-aged conductor, a
moustache like Harold's lawn – but this was music of a sort
and the Whittakers' piano with its moribund photographs
had been closed. Peter leant back on his bench to listen, a
proprietary foot on the rungs of the old pram.

It was 'doo da day' and 'oompa': a bizarre medley of
Strauss and Andrew Lloyd Weber, Elgar, 'Men of Harlech',
'Tipperary' and even 'Danny Boy'. Peter, arms loose at his
sides, legs stretched out, face open, dropped his father's notes
into his lap, thought how marvellous it must be to play even
in an orchestra such as this, to be there in an open anorak and
trainers, sweating in a nylon shirt, drinking a pint of best. He

tapped out the rhythm, his fingers, rather dirty now, on the handle of the pram. In some odd way we have to come through, he thought, with a benign peep at the contents of the pram; there is no other city, I am not unique, everyone who lives a little pushes a battered pram.

There was optimism in the air that Friday night and Peter, in the thick of it, breathed it in. *Au revoir, arriveaderci, bon voyage*, so long, farewell, hugging, kissing, waving; goodbye? The departures board whirred and clicked. Anxious travellers craned their necks to decipher and to see, trains came in and went out again to the crashing of the cymbals of the band. Peter with his pram, sitting beyond the rail bar on the bench, holding fast now to the music as if it were a rock, head above the waterline, coming up for air. 'Men of Harlech', 'Tipperary' 'Danny Boy', Worplesden, Shalford, Normandy? Now at last and not too late, he remembered something that he had forgotten, something between being emotionally incontinent and technically dead:

– 'The knee bone connected to the heart beat and heart beat connected to the head' –

Something the tiniest child can do that gets forgotten once one's frightened of looking like a fool. Something that he thought had gone under with his father in the Isle of Wight was there for Peter at Paddington, call collect, bobbing up through the detritus of the station, of the shore. Something that Joyce never had been capable of, something that Ralph had sought, something that Audrey had and Nicola, however well intentioned, could not reach. A mouth stuffed with bluebells – heart connected to the head – it was rapture and transportation, unwinding the arms, uncrossing the legs, not drowning but dancing, waving a hand and a leg. ' "Not to go back," ' he quoted aloud, ' "is somewhat to advance, and men must walk at least before they dance." '

On glue, thought the child-like woman in the waisted coat, giving a quick glance to Peter's jerky motion, foxtrot, as she dipped her hand into the rubbish bin for the discarded shaving brush, shoved it in her pocket, went on. 'Old enough to know better,' muttered a poorly shaven, passing punk.

147

'Call that dancing!' sneered a glossy woman with *Pineapple* spelt out across her breast. 'Just the ticket,' said the ringdoughnut face as Peter put a 50p into his collection box — just the ticket Peter needed, courtesy of the Western Region Military Band, the musical accompaniment for the journey towards B.

In the chill of the evening, Peter leant over the pram once more, took out the sleeve of his father's green, silk, paisley dressing gown and wound its comfort round his neck. What makes the eye slide? Departures announced the possibility of the inter-city westwards, 8.15.

The train to Cornwall and the west has no fairy lights nor even the attentions of Santayana, the Tolstoy two-step so very vivid in Peter's recurring dream; but heading westwards you can watch the red ball of the sun as it soaks the sky, fades, falls and finally sinks. 'Chilled drinks, toasted sandwiches, all-day breakfast' — and sunset all the way.

Also available in Pavanne

Grace Ingoldby's first novel:

Across the Water

Marking the debut of a remarkable new writer, *Across the Water* is a novel about its characters – a family tragedy set in Co. Fermanagh during the summer drought of 1976. It is about two brothers – Desmond and Boyle Hamilton – who were sent 'across the water' to England to be educated. Desmond escaped from his Northern Irish roots, married an English girl and has become a trendy playwright in London. Boyle, now forty, still lives with his 'Dada' in the dilapidated Georgian family house, isolated in his own world behind huge wrought-iron gates . . . Boyle is eccentric, close to madness, and he has maintained a friendship bordering on love with a seventeen-year-old Catholic youth suspected of complicity in the murder of their neighbour.

This murder is investigated by an English army officer who – as it turns out – was at school with Desmond and Boyle when they were 'across the water'. Desmond's wife Aimee arrives to spend the summer – she's bored, conventional, middle-class and very English – and she drifts into an affair with the Englishman. Desmond arrives to make a pretentious film about Irish Celtic twilight and the ancient tradition of a stone which sits on an island in the lake . . . the island where Boyle's disturbed mind will finally crack and where the inevitable tragedy will take place . . .

'A first novel of rare authority, steeped in menace' *Daily Telegraph*

'A strong, confident and original debut . . . a gripping account of people in whom violence erupts' *Cosmopolitan*

'A strongly imagined and accomplished first novel . . . a horrible family tragedy played out by people exhausted in the heat and made threadbare by old, unresolved conflicts' *Guardian*

'Accomplished and sure in its own right . . . you feel compelled to read on to the horrifying, beautifully described end'

Susan Hill, *Good Housekeeping*

'The wit is accurate and very funny; trenchant, but never dismissive'

Colin Greenland, *New Statesman*

THE ANDERSON QUESTION by Bel Mooney

Bel Mooney was born and brought up in Liverpool. As a philosophy student at London University, she met her future husband, the broadcaster Jonathan Dimbleby. They now live near Bath with their son and daughter. *The Windsurf Boy*, her first novel, reached the *Sunday Times* bestseller list. Bel Mooney has worked as a journalist for a wide variety of publications and has appeared regularly on television and radio. She is now a regular columnist on the *Sunday Times*, and reviews fiction for *Cosmopolitan*.

'A novelist of perceptive strength . . . Bel Mooney plots an authentic, compelling detective story of the soul' *Company*

Eleanor Anderson's comfortable and well-ordered life is completely shattered when her husband David, the dependable and much respected village doctor, disappears. A few days later he is found dead, apparently the victim of a heart attack, and speculation is stilled as family, friends and patients alike feel a kind of relief at knowing the worst.

But genuine grief at their bereavement gives way to angry bewilderment when a post-mortem reveals that the man they thought they knew so well, the man they all depended on, had taken his own life, for no obvious reason. And Eleanor discovers, in the uneasy company of her ungracious son, that all she had assumed and lived by has been false. . .

'She writes sensitively of a close village life, and tenderly of the anguish and soul-searching in his wife that Anderson's death provokes . . . it marks a real step forward in Bel Mooney's development as a remarkably good novelist'

Susan Hill, *Good Housekeeping*

'Beautifully written, compassionate . . . extremely moving . . . one of the best novels I have read for a long time' *Books and Bookmen*

BEYOND THE MOUNTAIN by Elizabeth Arthur

This is an extraordinary novel combining the passion surrounding an intense emotional relationship with vivid, descriptive travel writing.

Beyond the Mountain is the story of a woman mountaineer whose husband and brother have recently been killed in an avalanche. With them she formed a world famous trio of mountain climbers. Now, in an attempt to get over what has happened, she joins an all-women expedition in the Himalayas and, interspersed with the gruelling experience of the ascent, which incorporates some extraordinary writing about mountaineering, she is forced to come to terms with the past, her grief, and ultimately the fact that her marriage was an extremely difficult one.

  The action is played out against the snow-capped peaks of the Himalayas and the stark reality of that horizon contrasts emphatically with the woman's confusion regarding her dead brother and husband.

'Elizabeth Arthur does something very special in her writing; she handles brutal realism and finely crafted fiction as one medium. The background to her story is thoroughly researched. One can hear the crunch of her feet in the snow, feel the cold and battle with her at the same time in the complex realm of emotions. She deals with desire, fear, guilt and love with compelling honesty, painting them in strong primary colours and skipping the pastel hues – but she also manages to be poetic and all the way through the balance between physical and emotional drama is beautifully achieved. She never goes over the top.'

Lucy Irvine, author of
Castaway

'For myself as a traveller, I particularly appreciated her vividly evocative descriptions of the Nepalese scene. The novel blends a matter-of-fact earthiness with the emotional turmoil of a distressed person, set against a background of mountain-climbing – lucid and incisive, with sensitive insights into character relationships.'

Christina Dodwell, author of
In Papua New Guinea

'A densely woven, ambitious book. Its concerns and characters, its lyricism and sculpted form will speak to and impress the sensitive reader . . . Uniquely memorable' *The Washington Post*

'The story is as stunning – as stark and subtle – as the blue-and-white landscape that enhances these people' *The New Yorker*

VIRGIN TERRITORY by Sara Maitland

Rape: a traumatic experience for any woman, a particular crisis for a nun. Sister Kitty's rape affects all the members of her South American community. She survives. But Sister Anna comes close to a nervous breakdown and it is suggested that she should take a year's sabbatical to recover.

So Sister Anna is sent to London, where she becomes involved in a very different kind of life. Her time is spent studying in the British Library, and helping a couple with their brain-damaged child. Then she meets Karen, a gay feminist, who introduces Anna to a new world, new ideas and new values. For the first time in her life – in her mid-thirties – she is independent, free to listen and to choose. She finds herself in turn excited, challenged, threatened, and eventually forced to reassess her own vocation: what, in the face of rape, and the challenging roles of women, can her virginity mean now?

The subject of Sara Maitland's second novel is powerful and she writes boldly, richly and evocatively. With her first novel, *Daughter of Jerusalem*, she won the Somerset Maugham Award. Her short stories have equally received high critical acclaim. Now *Virgin Territory* confirms that she is one of the most talented and original writers to emerge from the British Women's Movement.

'A challenging and joyful book by an extraordinarily gifted writer'
Books and Bookmen

'The pressures on Anna are extreme – bullying voices of the Church Fathers in her head, the destructive empathy with a brain-damaged child she cares for, and the temptation of physical love with another woman . . . This closely argued polemical novel contains some striking truths that are not often aired'
Daily Telegraph